## HOMECOMING

"Well now, it's McCool, ain't it?" The bull-necked man fingered the Colt at his hip as he stepped up and grinned. "Mr. Hughson told me to explain that hell-raisers like you ain't needed here in Texas. You savvy?"

Rian McCool started his swing as he pivoted. His fist came around like a rock...

Across the street, a hoarse cry sounded: "McCool's back!"

### CAST A LONG SHADOW

### FRANK BONHAM

# FRANK BONHAM

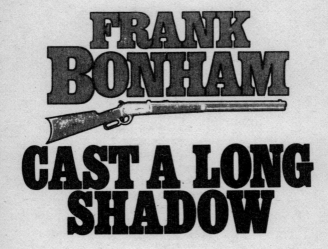

# CAST A LONG SHADOW

BERKLEY BOOKS, NEW YORK

CAST A LONG SHADOW

A Berkley Book / published by arrangement with
the author

PRINTING HISTORY
Monarch Books edition / May 1964
Berkley edition / March 1980
Second printing / February 1982

ISBN: 0-425-05229-X

A BERKLEY BOOK ® TM 757,375
PRINTED IN THE UNITED STATES OF AMERICA

# CAST A LONG SHADOW

# Chapter One

VALLECITO WAS A swing stop on the stage line from the West Texas border to the Panhandle. In ten minutes teams were changed, passengers and mail dealt with, and the stage sent rolling on across the flinty range land. The dust of the northbound's arrival had hardly settled that October day when the shotgun guard blew his copper bugle and the coach swung from the depot and on up the shallow canyon of dun-colored buildings into the prairie...

The passenger who had arrived from Kingbolt with no luggage, and a Colt on his hip, came from the washroom behind the station. His name was Artie Judd. He was big, somnolent and slow-moving, not a cowboy by his look, not a businessman—a hard type to peg. He wore a shirt of striped material, like a barber's apron, lavender sleeve-garters, and black trousers stuffed into his boots—on the inner side, Texas style. He looked neither lean enough nor stove-up enough to be a cowpuncher, nor did he appear sufficiently harried to be a rancher in that corner of Texas, where it took a section of grass to fatten a couple of dozen cows.

He walked up to the stationmaster, who was talking to a paunchy, middle-aged man, put his boot on the hub of a wagon, and looked at them. The heavy-set man, who wore a star, glanced at him with cautious interest. He had a yellowish, jaded and somehow sad face.

"Something?" asked the stationmaster.

"What time does the Kingbolt stage come through?" Judd asked.

The stationmaster smiled. "Kingbolt? You just came from there, mister."

The sheriff punched the stage man lightly on the shoulder. "See you later, Howie. Got to feed the animals." He strolled down the boardwalk toward a blocklike building sitting by itself at the front of a large lot.

Judd said to the stationmaster, "All right. I just came from there. In an hour I'll finish my business and head back. When's the stage?"

The other man looked at a silver pocket-watch. "Hour and a half. Do you want a ticket?"

"I've got a ticket—traveling round-trip. What about the westbound stage?"

"To El Paso?"

"To Arizona."

"Same stage. Comes through about five o'clock tonight."

2

"How much is the fare to Tucson?"

"I'd have to look it up."

Judd waved a hand toward the station. The stage man, with a frown of irritation, went into the building. Judd followed. At his desk, the agent donned spectacles and consulted a schedule.

"Sixty dollars," he said, glancing up.

"Gimme a ticket. One way."

"From here?"

Judd sighed and placed both hands on the man's desk. "If you'd been born any slower, you'd'a been a desert turtle! One ticket *from here*. That is correct. Reckon you can get it written up before five o'clock?"

For a moment the stationmaster's eyes grew tart; then, after a better look into Judd's hard, fleshy features, he muttered and began writing up the ticket.

Artie Judd paid the fare with three gold double-eagles. He folded the ticket and slipped it into the pocket of his striped shirt. But as the other man turned away, Judd caught his arm.

"Oh, uh—know a man named McCool?"

The stationmaster, his face frozen with dislike, said, "I know three men named McCool. Two are in the cemetery and one's in jail."

"The one I want is named Rian."

"You're in luck. That's the live one."

"Live as ever?" Judd said, with a grin.

"Hard to say. Tell better when he hits the street. He was live enough when he went in a year ago. Lord knows the McCools were always live enough for three men, once they'd put away a couple of whiskies. You a friend of Rian's?"

3

Frowning faintly, Artie Judd pursed his lips. "You might say so. I want to do him a favor. I reckon that makes me a friend, don't it?"

The agent shrugged, and Judd went to the door. For some reason, the agent looked at the gun on Judd's hip. It had the prettiest grips he had ever seen: tortoise shell, with a silver design countersunk into them. The sun glowed amber through the tortoise shell as the man from Kingbolt walked into the light. Artie Judd tucked his hands under his belt and strolled up the street.

In the jail office, as he entered, Sheriff Charlie Crump was just sitting down with a heavy china cup of coffee. A fragrance of chili beans hung in the air, but no food was in sight; Judd supposed he had just fed his prisoners—"the animals," as he called them. The sheriff glanced at him.

"Hello," he said, with dry disinterest.

"George Hughson wrote you about me, sheriff. I'm Artie Judd."

"Allowed you were."

"You can turn McCool loose any time now," Judd said.

"I can, eh?" said the sheriff ironically, looking again at Judd. "You tell Hughson something for me when you go back. I don't like his way of doing things. I've held McCool a week beyond his sentence on your boss man's say. If he wanted a welcome-home committee on hand when McCool got out, why couldn't he send somebody up on time?"

"Somebody?" Judd smiled. "That would be me. I

was busy. First chance I've had to get up here. You'll get your campaign contribution, so what's eating on you?"

"Superintendent!" snorted the sheriff. "You don't look like no stage man to me. What do you know about horses and rolling stock?"

Judd rubbed his chin. "I work more with people," he said. "Mr. Hughson takes care of the other details."

The sheriff drank some coffee and set the cup down. "What kind of shenanigans are you planning?"

"The boss man said to bring McCool his regards."

"Why couldn't the boss man bring them himself?"

"He's busy with his new stage line."

Crump snorted. "Busy running it into the ground, I hear."

Judd regarded him for a moment, then touched the brim of his hat. "Take care, Sheriff. Ready any time you are. Oh—keep his gun. You can send it to him in Arizona."

"Why Arizona?"

"Because that's where he's going from here."

# Chapter Two

RIAN MCCOOL LAY on the jail cot, smoking
the cigar he had found on his lunch tray. One arm
kinked under his head, he gazed thoughtfully at the
ceiling, luxuriously blowing smoke at the beams. He
half expected the cigar to explode. On the other
hand, he took the gift of a cigar to be significant.
Maybe he was going to be turned loose today. In the
week since he figured he should have been released,
Sheriff Crump had surprised him with a number of
little favors, despite their running argument about
when his sentence ended. Hard man to figure out.

McCool's finger traced a series of penciled marks
on the wall above his bed. It had pleased him to
defile public property in this way; also, it had
enabled him to count the days. McCool was

twenty-three, an inch under six feet and large-boned. He had a snub nose and a wide mouth, with reddish-brown hair that needed cutting. Though his color was pasty from long confinement, he was in good physical condition. He had seen men dissolve into wheezy fatness when they suddenly gave over heavy work to which they were accustomed. Twice a day he had chinned himself on the bars and managed what exercise he could in such tight quarters.

McCool suddenly raised his voice. "Hey, Sheriff!"

A barred door opened and the sheriff came plodding to his cell. "What's the problem?"

With the cigar, the prisoner pointed at the marks on the wall. "I just counted them again. I'm seven days overtime already!"

Crump smiled. "How much ciphering did you have in school, Rian?"

"Enough to learn to count the days in a year."

"Maybe this was leap year."

Knocking ash on the floor, McCool said, "I'll sue you for every extra day you hold me."

"That's fair enough. How much do you figure your valuable time is worth?"

"Fifty dollars a day."

"Is that what George Hughson paid you to break horses for his stage line?" the sheriff asked.

"Don't forget, I had a ranch, too, when I came here."

Crump laughed. "So you did. A ranch that lost so much money you had to close up and break horses to pay your taxes! How's the stogey?" he asked.

Rian looked at it thoughtfully. "I keep wondering how I'll look with powder burns on my face."

"It's a two-bit cigar, son. A going-away present."

Rian rolled to his feet and hastened to the barred door. "Am I getting out?"

With a sad smile, the sheriff nodded. "Any minute now. Rian, I'm sorry—I did hold you past your time. But I was afraid to let you out till your attitude improved."

"My *what*?" Rian stared at him.

"The way you felt about things. Take it from me—if you hit the sidewalk looking for George Hughson to square with him for testifying against you, you'll be back before the horned toads hibernate. Don't do it, Rian. You lost a little time. But you're young. You can make a new start."

McCool took a deep breath. Already his lungs seemed to expand more freely. "My sentence didn't include listening to advice from you," he said. "That would be what they called 'cruel and unusual punishment,' wouldn't it?"

Crump's jaundiced eyes blinked slowly. "Well, you're kind of an unusual prisoner. Got it from your father, I reckon. Or your older brother—may his brawler's soul rest in peace. Unusualness kind of runs in your family, seems like. Every time your father got tanked up, he'd get so unusual it took a dozen men to subdue him so I could arrest him."

Rian turned away to start collecting the few small possessions he had been allowed to keep with him. Pulling a box from under his cot, he threw a frowning glance at the lawman.

"Why didn't you jug some of the men that put

him up to his foolishness? Like Tom Baker. Baker got bounced out of Cloverleaf for taking liberties with a bar girl in the sight of the whole saloon. He couldn't make an issue of it, him being a bank manager, or it would have gotten back to his wife. So he told my Old Man the bouncer had been saying he could whip any McCool, including him, with one hand."

Crump frowned. "Is that the way it happened?" he said, seemingly surprised and disturbed.

"That's the way it happened," Rian said doggedly. "The Old Man couldn't let a slur like that pass, so he came charging into the Cloverleaf and the bouncer belted him with a pool cue. Self-defense."

Crump massaged his flabby cheeks with his fingertips. "It *was* self-defense. Everybody saw your father start the fight."

"A bouncer ought to be able to subdue a sixty-year-old man without a club. Without killing him, at least. Ah, hell—forget it," McCool sighed. "I had some money when I came here. Do I get it back?"

"You'll get it," Sheriff Crump said with a sigh. "About twenty bucks. Pack your stuff while I unlock my safe."

"Wait a minute," McCool said. He walked to the door and gazed earnestly into the lawman's face. "Can I ask you something, off the record?"

"Why not?"

"You don't really think I made that stage team bolt, do you?"

"What's the difference? At the trial you didn't

seem to know yourself what you'd done. You were too drunk that night to hit the ground with your hat. It's done and past. Forget it."

Packing, Rian tried to penetrate the black fog of that night which had changed his life. He remembered clearly the start of it and the end. The end was right here. The start was in a restaurant where he and Abby Burland had had dinner.

Abby was a pretty, gray-eyed widow who was trying to operate a ranch and showing no talent for ranching whatever. Rian soon found the troubles he'd acquired since his father's death augmented by one more complication: he was in love.

At first it had seemed like wonderful good fortune. He and Abby talked about marriage, and a house near town. Rian was breaking horses for George Hughson at the time, while waiting for some of his beef cattle to mature so that he could raise cash for his new year's operations. About all he'd been left at his father's death was a big silver watch and a hatful of delinquent bills.

Though neither he nor Abby had much in the way of land, together they would have had something to build on. He'd reached the point of wondering whether the tiny diamond ring his mother had left on her death ten years ago was a suitable engagement ring.

So that night at the restaurant he produced the ring—duly polished with baking soda—and tried to slip it on her finger. Abby rejected it, startled, then angry. She glanced around, hoping no one had seen. Then she went outside.

He followed her, dazed. "What's wrong, Abby?"

"Well, if you don't know—! Good heavens! I don't mind being *friends* with you but—"

Ice began to form in Rian McCool's belly. "What do you mean?"

The idea, it appeared, was that roughhousing and violent death seemed to be occupational hazards of the McCool clan; that it had been rather embarrassing to keep company with him, but she had been lonesome since her husband's death. And that she had been seeing George Hughson lately and—

Shaking with rage and hurt, Rian turned his back and walked off.

At eleven o'clock that night, Rian had traded his mother's engagement ring for the last round of drinks at the saloon, and staggered off to the stage station to find his cot in the harness room, where he was bunking while he broke horses.

Something was going on at the stage depot that night; something he had not been able to cipher out in a year of puzzling.

He recalled seeing the night mail-stage to Alamos, a little four-horse Troy coach, waiting in the yard. There were seldom any passengers for the run. Biff Shackley, the driver, stood beside it in the darkness, apparently ready to travel.

What stopped Rian was the strange light in the stage office—an eerie, flickering blue glow. Even in his drunken state, he was puzzled. There was something peculiar in Shackley's silence, too. He'd never hit it off with Shackley, a glowering bull of a man who doubled as superintendent and once-a-week night driver. But, full of whiskey, Rian forgave him all his failings.

He pulled a pint bottle from his pocket and shook it. The bottle gurgled, so he knew there was some liquor left. He raised it, toastlike, toward Shackley.

"Biff," he called, starting forward. "Hey, Biff— hair of the dog, ole buddy?"

Then he saw the light in the stage station flare higher, and he stopped and stared at it. "Holy cow, Biff—is that a fire in there?" he croaked.

There was an earsplitting explosion beside his head. Orange light blinded him. He heard the horses squeal and stampede out of the yard, with Shackley yelling, "Ho, fools—ho, there!"

An instant later, something landed heavily on Rian's head and that was the end of his evening.

The charge was tampering with U. S. mails, firing a gun in the city limits, being drunk and disorderly. One of the horses had to be destroyed when it stumbled and broke a leg. He could have gotten ten years in Leavenworth. Because he was drunk, he got off with a year.

But what had been going on at the station that night? He had blundered into something. When, on the witness stand, he tried to explain his impressions—the blue light and all—the jury smiled. Alcoholic hallucinations. Nevertheless, he'd like about an hour with George Hughson or Biff Shackley to talk about it.

For Hughson, too, it had been quite a year: taking over the old McCool place at a delinquent tax sale; marrying Abby Burland and acquiring her ranch; selling both of them, and his stage line, and moving to a booming new area on the border, of which Kingbolt was the heart. A big—suspiciously big—year.

You couldn't argue with success, they said. But you could sit down quietly with a man and ask him some questions about how he got successful so fast. This was the first order of business on McCool's calendar— the *only* order, for a man with no money and few talents.

"I'll have to keep your gun, Rian," the sheriff explained as he returned Rian's money and possessions.

"Why?"

"It's the law. You'll get it back in a week. If you should leave town, drop me a card from where you're going."

McCool shrugged. Maybe just as well, he thought. After all, the name's still McCool. "So long, Sheriff," he said.

"So long, Rian. Luck, son."

## Chapter Three

RIAN STEPPED INTO the sunlight and looked
at the world. It was beautiful—a clear sky as blue as
Indian turquoise; a warm breeze blowing against his
face, and miles and miles of open prairie beyond the
town. He felt tears fill his eyes. Turning his face up,
he let the warm sky pour down on him like a
waterfall.

After a moment, carrying his belongings in a roll
under his arm, he started toward the stage station.
He knew the schedule—it was nearly all he did know
about the world, these days—and he wanted to see
how far his twenty dollars would take him.

"Well, what do you know?" a man said. "So
that's the great McCool."

Rian halted. The man lounged in a recessed

window of an adobe building. He was big, bluntly made, with a buttoned collarband shirt of striped material, but no necktie. At his hip was a Colt with striking tortoiseshell grips. The gun made Rian think of the empty holster he carried rolled under his arm. Bullnecked and solid, the stranger had eyebrows thickened with scar tissue like a pug's. He stood up and grinned at Rian.

"It *is* McCool, ain't it?"

"That's right. Who are you?"

"Name of Judd. I work for Frontier Stage Lines. George Hughson sent me. I've got something for you."

Rian's principal emotion was one of disappointment. So that was why Charlie Crump had held him past the day of his release! The sheriff was not exactly a clear-eyed fighting lawman, but Rian had not believed him capable of setting up something like this. He knew now why his gun had not been returned.

Artie Judd handed him a slip of paper, and he took it. It was a printed ticket, with *Tucson, A.T.*, written on it in violet ink. He tucked it into his shirt pocket.

"Thanks," he said, starting on.

"Judd put himself in his path. "Not so fast. Are you going?"

"Sure, I'm going."

Again Judd had to block his way. The burly straw boss seemed perplexed that he had not had more trouble with him.

"The stage is at five o'clock," he said sullenly.

16

"Not my stage," Rian said. "It'll be along in about an hour. I'm going to Kingbolt. I'll turn this one in on it and have about thirty dollars left, I should reckon."

Judd's eyes whetted. On the rim of his vision, Rian could see a few townsmen across the street watching him. He wondered about the sheriff. Had he locked up and ridden away in order not to be dragged into whatever was coming?

Judd caught a thumb in his cartridge belt and rested his hand above his Colt. "Mr. Hughson told me to explain that if you ever come back to Texas, he'll take it to mean you're armed. Because hell-raisers like you ain't needed here. You savvy?"

Rian nodded. "You bet. Thanks, Judd. Nice talking to you."

Again he started toward the stage station. This time Judd's thick fingers closed on his arm and yanked him back.

"Wait a minute, McCool!"

Rian started his swing as he pivoted. His fist came around like a rock whirled at the end of a cord. It smacked into the gunman's mouth with a meaty sound. Judd floundered back into the wall, his mouth loose, eyes out of focus. Blood smeared his wide-spaced front teeth.

Rian did not wait for him to recover. Judd was there to provoke a fight; he carried a gun and had seen to it that Rian did not. As the gunman shook his head to clear it, Rian yanked the gun from its holster and tossed it into the street.

Across the way, a man bawled hoarsely,

"McCool's out!" A horse stamped nervously at a hitchrack. A child screeched and ran down a boardwalk.

Big and indestructible, Artie Judd suddenly collected himself and lunged from the wall. Sliding away, Rian smashed a blow to the side of his head and followed it with a fist dug into his kidney. Judd whirled to follow him. He threw a backhand smash at Rian which collided with the side of his head.

Rian's vision blurred. His knees started to give way.

Judd was upon him savagely, ripping short, hard blows at his head. Rian fell, but instantly rolled under a hitchrack and into the street as Judd tried to kick him. He could see the legs of the man who had collected to watch the brawl. He scrambled up, breathless and dazed, the objects around him touched with a soap-bubble shimmer. He saw the gunman duck under the rail to follow him.

Stepping in quickly, Rian drove his knee into Judd's face while he was bent over. Judd sprawled back onto the walk. A pain in Rian's chest stabbed him every time he breathed, making him gasp. One way or another, he knew, this fight was about over.

He ducked under the rack and was set in a wide stance when Judd floundered up, his bloody mouth cursing. Rage shook his judgment. He drove in wildly. Rian ducked under his flailing arms and brought a fist up under his jaw to turn Judd's face up to the sun. The big man's whole body loosened. While he seemed to hang there, McCool sank his fist into his belly, straightened him again with a looping

uppercut, then hammered a right with all he had
into the massive jaw.

Judd fell back, his arms dropping. His heel
caught and he sprawled backward on the walk. He
rolled over, hunched up as if to rise, then groaned
and relaxed.

Rian slumped against the wall of a building and
closed his eyes while the world revolved about him.

When he boarded the stage that afternoon, a
handsome Colt gleamed in his holster—Artie
Judd's. He had washed up, rested on his old cot, and
by stage time was functioning again. He did not see
Judd, though he had expected to. A realist, McCool
told himself: *I'll see him in Kingbolt*. No doubt
about that. Judd, who obviously made his living
with a gun, would have to clean up this unfinished
business before he could conscientiously resume his
trade of journeyman gunman.

All Rian hoped was to see George Hughson and
Biff Shackley first.

The afternoon passed in a series of dusty
crossroads towns, the sun burning in from the west
as the coach traveled toward the border. Rian
dozed, awakening when they made a meal stop at
sundown.

Ahead, the gullied scenery was breaking up into
mountains. Somewhere beyond the mountains was
the Big River, and Mexico. He had never been to
Kingbolt, but he knew it was on the north bank of
the river, and did a prosperous trade with the mines

and the ranch communities across the border.

During the night the coach slowed as the road roughened and began to climb. He slept fitfully. Once, it seemed to him that Abby Burland—Abby *Hughson*, rather—sat beside him. She was weeping quietly. "I'm sorry I hurt you, Rian. I shouldn't have led you on—" Another time she was laughing. He had seldom heard her laugh, for she was usually grave, almost shy. And her lips were as red as a saloon girl's when she laughed in harsh mockery.

"You thought I'd marry *you*? You idiot, Rian! You're just as crazy as all the others of your family, aren't you? Oh, excuse me—there aren't any others in your family now, are there? Your face, Rian! It's a scream. You're puckered up to cry, like a little boy."

The curious thing was that there were tears in his eyes when he awoke.

He had the strangest feeling that while he slept he had been given the vision to see her as she truly was; that she had seen the moment coming when he would give her a ring, and had relished it.

Lots to settle in Kingbolt, he thought.

# Chapter Four

IN A COOL, windy dawn, the stagecoach halted at a small town high in the mountains. Beyond the buildings, Rian glimpsed small cedars and piñons bathed in pink light. There was a pleasant taste of wood smoke in the air. Stiff and tired, he trudged into the station with the other passengers and had a breakfast of flinty corn bread and fried fat-pork. A baggage counter spanned one wall, with a hog-wire partition forming an office at one end of it. Two men stood behind the partition. Rian could hear them talking.

"Now, your petty cash should *never* be counted with the rest," one man was saying. "Otherwise you're counting it twice, don't you see? And this—this item here—"

The speaker was a small man wearing a bowler hat and a suit as black and shiny as a blackbird's wing. He looked energetic and compact, with the wiriness of a man who might have swung a double-bitted axe in his younger years. He seemed to be showing his companion, an older man, how to keep his post-office accounts straight. Probably a postal inspector, Rian conjectured.

When the conductor said, "Five minutes, folks!" the man in the black suit said quickly, "That's it, Henry. You're doing fine. Don't let my nit-picking upset you." He laughed and slapped the postmaster on the back.

Several passengers boarded for Kingbolt. Since it was going to be crowded inside, McCool climbed to the hurricane deck, taking the seat behind the driver. Soon the postal inspector joined him.

"Man alive! Too crowded down there to breathe without jostlin' somebody." He smiled at Rian and offered his hand. "Sylvester Morton." Two gold teeth gleamed when he smiled.

"Rian McCool."

The stage ran on. "Where to?" Morton asked Rian.

"Kingbolt."

"Locating there?"

"Hard to say."

Morton drew a flat bottle of liquor from his coat pocket. He uncorked it, started to drink, then offered it to Rian. "Have a drink?"

Remembering his last drink, Rian shook his head. Morton again started to drink, realized the coach was jouncing so hard he would probably chip a tooth, and frowned. He leaned forward to tap the driver on the shoulder.

"Matt—hand 'em in a bit, eh?"

"Yes, sir. You bet, Mr. Morton," the driver said. He pulled the horses in to a walk.

Rian was pleasantly startled. Ask a stage driver to slow his team for your comfort? Not if you valued your health. At best, you would probably be put off the stage. It gave Rian insight into the power of a postal inspector to bestow or take away mail franchises.

"All right. Thanks," the little man said, and the horses hit the collars again.

"What kind of work do you do?" he asked Rian.

For an instant, Rian was irritated by the man's inquisitiveness. Yet it seemed to grow from genuine interest in him, perhaps a liking. He relaxed.

"I'm a rancher. That is—I was a rancher. My last job was breaking horses for a stage line."

"You're a shade pale for a man who works outdoors."

Rian set his jaw and stared down the road. It swept into a high, rocky pass beyond which he knew there would be a valley. "It's a long story, friend."

"Say no more," said Morton. "I was prying— can't help it sometimes. Reckon I just like people. I was thinking, though," he added, "that if you'd just come out of the hospital, say, I might be able to speak to one of my business acquaintances about you, help you get lined up with a job."

"Thanks anyway. I'm only going to be around a week or so. Collect some money a man owes me, and take off."

Morton leaned toward him, his breath spiced with liquor. "The man wouldn't be Arthur Judd, would he?" At Rian's astounded expression, Morton slapped his thigh and laughed.

Then Rian remembered the gun in his holster. He glanced down at it.

Morton chuckled. "I know George Hughson well, and I've met Artie Judd. What in the world are you doing with his gun?"

In the end, Rian told him most of the story.

"So you're going to Kingbolt to kill Hughson," Morton said gravely.

"No, that's not the idea at all. I'm going to demand some of the money he owes me. He bought my ranch for back taxes, after scaring off all the other possible buyers who might have paid me a fair price. I figure that if he's nervous enough, he might pay me a thousand dollars to go away. He must be nervous, or he wouldn't have sent Judd to flag me off."

"Bosh. You're going there in the hope that Hughson will provoke a fight and you can kill him. You're thinking with your hands, not your head, McCool," he sighed.

"Maybe that's the best way, for a man with a fourth grade education."

Morton was silent. At last he said, "You've come to a fork in the trail, McCool. I came to a fork once, myself..." Rian did not prod him; he did not have to. Morton was merely pondering it carefully. "Well, that's neither here nor there. The fact is, you strike me as a man of ability and determination. I hate to see you point your compass in the wrong direction and lose your way."

"It points to Kingbolt, Mr. Morton."

"All right! Agreed. But use your wits. You want your money—you want to square with a man. That's fine. But don't kill him. Break him!"

Rian studied him, frowning. "How?"

"Well . . . for example—you might take a job with Hughson's competitor. Hughson doesn't have a mail contract, you know. But he's trying hard for one, and if he doesn't get it, he'll probably go under."

"Who does have it?"

"Man named Reese—Dan Reese. Churchly old citizen. Not geared for running a stage line in a growing country. His daughter's the businessman of the family, I suspect. But he was there first, and he's had the franchise for years. Then Hughson came. He offered to buy Reese out, but the old man refused. So Hughson went in competition. He's already taken over most of the business. Whatever else you can say about George Hughson, he gets the job done—which is more than the Reeses are doing, unfortunately."

Rian smiled wryly. "So I take a job breaking horses for Dan Reese. How does that hurt Hughson?"

Morton sighed. Lowering his voice, he said, "I can't take sides in the awarding of a mail contract, you understand. In fact, when Reese's franchise comes up for renewal, I may have to recommend termination in favor of Hughson's line. *But—*" he raised his forefinger portentously— "suppose you took a job with the Reeses and got their line moving again. Then I'd be justified in approving their renewal."

Rian rubbed his jaw, a warm interest spreading through him. "I see..."

With a dry chuckle, the postal inspector said, "Hughson *might* be able to sell out before his creditors pounced. But I doubt it. Just between you and me, he and his lovely young wife are up to their eyeballs in debt."

The stage topped a divide. Below them spread a wide and golden plain. In the heart of it, a river glinted in a haze of greenery. A few miles south of the mountains lay a town, its environs patterned with irrigated fields. Smoke hung above the area.

Excitement began to pound in McCool. *Hughson and his lovely wife."* A chance to hang the man's hide on a fence—to show Abby that the name McCool did not necessarily imply stupidity and impoverishment.

Morton was saying, "Of course, you'd have to make a deal with the Reeses. Can't expect to break horses or drive for them and make any money. Insist on a partnership."

Rian bit his lip. The rub, always the rub. But a partnership with what? "I've got fifty-one-dollars, Mr. Morton," he sighed.

"And Artie Judd's gun. The Reeses need that more than they need money. They've had a lot of hard luck with their rolling stock: coaches running off the grade, horses getting lost. Maybe it's just coincidence. But a young man able to disarm Artie Judd might be able to pull them through. Like to see you try," he said.

Rian drew the gun and looked at it. When he cocked it, the hammer would not stay back; the sear had been filed off for fast firing. He reholstered the gun.

Morton removed his black bowler hat. From the lining he drew a little leather packet of business cards. He extracted one and returned the rest. "I'll write a few words on this when the stage stops," he said. "Show it to Dan Reese—no, to his daughter. She's the brains of the outfit. Maybe it'll help."

As Rian looked at the little white pasteboard which could make a total change in his life, a warmth of gratitude spilled through him. He gripped Morton's hand.

"Mr. Morton, I—I don't know how—"

Morton drew his hand away, embarrassed. "Tut, tut! Just pointing out things you're too close to to see for yourself. Will you take one more word of advice?"

Rian nodded, his eyes eager.

Morton's chin tilted up a little, his voice grew sonorous. "Be true to yourself—decide what you're going to do, *then don't let anything stop you.* Nothing! Nobody in this world really gives a damn whether you sink or swim; that's the big lesson. So see to it that faint-heartedness doesn't betray you when the chips are down."

It was a little bewildering. Rian was not sure he got the message. But the words, *Be true to yourself,* burned in his mind like the after-image of a strong light stared at too long.

*By God!* he thought. *I never have been true to myself. I've let them discount me—even in my own eyes.* He seemed to glimpse success like a candle at the end of a long corridor lined by a hundred dark and sinister doors. He felt absolutely sure of reaching the end of the corridor.

At the first swing-stop, Morton scribbled on the back of the card and handed it to Rian.

*This will introduce Mr. Rian McCool, a personal friend. Any favor extended to him will be a favor to me...*

At last the stage road hit the valley and they rushed through golden, stirrup-high grass toward a town a couple of miles ahead. Morton leaned toward him.

"After you get lined up with a job, tear up the card. Wouldn't make me look good if anybody asked *why* I gave it to you. You and I know it's an act of friendship, right?"

"Of course." Rian said, nodding.

Morton pulled a buckskin purse from his pocket, glanced into it and gave an embarrassed laugh. "Pshaw! How do you like that? Two dollars in my pocket! I've got a rather large check in my valise, but I hate to hit a postmaster with it. And the bank will be closed." He closed the purse with a snap.

"Say! As long as we'll both be around town until I leave on the eleven o'clock stage, maybe you'd loan me fifty dollars for the evening? I'll meet you at the Pastime Bar at ten-thirty and pay you back. By that time I'll run into somebody who'll cash it without any embarrassment to me."

Fifty dollars! Rian knew he had only fifty-one dollars in his pocket. He hesitated. Either this little man was a liar and a fraud, or he was a magician who had touched his future with gold. For fifty dollars he could find out.

"What the hell!" he said. "For a friend?" He dug the coins from his pocket, finding he had nearly two dollars left after giving Morton the fifty.

The postal inspector slapped Rian's knee as he pocketed the money. "Good boy," he said.

Now the stage was rolling into the heart of a booming adobe metropolis. It slowed for the traffic of buggies, pedestrians, and dogs. Many Mexicans were on the street in their huge *jipi*-straw sombreros and white pajamalike clothing. Freight wagons rumbled along the scarred dirt streets, while cowboys jogged aside and a dray loaded with beer barrels pulled over to let the coach rattle past. On the walks were well-dressed ladies and businessmen in dark suits.

Rian cringed. This was a prosperous town, with many irons in the fire. And Rian McCool, jailbird and horse-breaker, was going to try to bluff it! He had nothing to sell but nerve. Inwardly, he quaked.

The stage rocked to a halt in a stage yard. Rian glanced at Morton, needing reassurance. The little man smiled and whispered:

"'This above all—to thine own self be true—!'"

They gripped hands. "Ten-thirty—Pastime Bar!" said Morton.

Rian breathed deeply. Then, with no baggage but Artie Judd's six-gun, he dropped down and set his feet in the earth of his new life.

# Chapter Five

WAITING NERVOUSLY IN their town buggy, the Hughsons saw the stagecoach coming down the street. "There it is!" Abby Hughson exclaimed. She was a small, beautifully formed girl with creamy skin and lustrous black hair. Her skin was naturally tawny, her teeth very white.

At her side, her husband glanced impatiently at her. "For God's sake, don't sound so eager," he said. "We're here to ask Morton to dinner. He isn't the President, you know."

Abby looked at him reproachfully. "Perhaps I'm eager because it's my money we stand to lose if we go under."

George Hughson smiled. He was tall and muscular in a gray suit, with a dove-gray Stetson

31

placed on the side of his head. He wore a neat dark mustache. There was a look of solidness to George Hughson, an air of importance and reliability. But Abby had seen the mask come off. In the bedroom, that first night, and every time he toted up profits and losses and realized that with all his solidness and deep-voiced bluff, he was losing ground in this too-fast-paced gamble.

Hughson said in a pleasant, almost affectionate voice, "Oh, come now, Abby. You know better than that. 'Your' money? Not according to the laws of the great State of Texas. It's *our* money, ever since the first night I took you to bed."

His language embarrassed her; for an instant her eyes fell. Looking at her hands clenched in her lap, she said, "I'm glad you've said it, at last. That was the only reason you married me, wasn't it? For a grubstake."

Hughson chuckled. "Let's just say that if *two* girls like you had thrown themselves at me—equally pretty—I'd have married the one with the ranch. In other words, I didn't hold your ranch against you."

Tears filled her eyes as she looked up. "I suppose you think you could divorce me now and leave me with nothing but a settlement. Well, you can't!"

Hughson sighed. "Don't be silly. And for God's sake, don't get your eyes and nose red, or you'll tout Morton off coming to dinner. You're going to feed him and laugh at his backwoods jokes—that's your department. Then he's going to have brandy and cigars and play a little poker—that's mine. And when he leaves, we can practically list a mail contract among our assets."

Abby sniffed. "You said that six months ago. But the Reeses are still in business. An old man and a girl—are they too much for you, George?"

Hughson, smiling, rested his hand on her leg. Abby caught her breath as his fingers dug into the nerves above her knee.

"I can handle the Reeses if you do your part. I handled McCool, didn't I? Now, are you going to dry your eyes and charm Mr. Morton?"

Abby's mouth had dropped open as she stared at the coach swinging into the yard in a nutmeg fog of dust. "*George!*" she whispered.

Hughson twisted to stare at the coach. Then he saw Rian McCool standing up as he prepared to dismount.

"That idiot, Judd!" he groaned. He bit his lip, thinking quickly. "All right—nothing's changed. I'll deal with McCool. Morton's coming to dinner. That's all that concerns you. Ready?"

She looked at him for strength. Some of her shock dissipated as she saw his coolness. He stepped down and reached a hand up to help her.

As she stepped onto the boardwalk, an elderly man and a young woman hurried by them into the stage yard. Daniel Reese and Justina—there on the same business that brought the Hughsons. Hughson chuckled as he gazed after them.

"God help Morton! They're probably going to rope him and drag him off like a steer! Why don't you wait here?" he suggested. "There's no use in our looking too eager."

For a moment there was confusion in the stage yard, the tired team being unlatched from the tugs, baggage being unearthed from the rear luggage boot, the express box tossed down by the conductor. A dozen townsmen had gathered to meet travelers or to watch the excitement. In this crowd, Hughson found it easy to take a place beside Justina Reese, out of Abby's view. When the girl glanced at him, he smiled and tipped his hat.

"Meeting someone, Miss Justina?"

"Oh, not really. Just looking for a package." The girl smiled. She hated him, he knew, but she wouldn't let her feelings show. She was a girl who knew how to play her cards.

Hughson liked that about her. She was really quite lovely, too: a reddish blonde with braids arranged like plaited gold wire, and the golden look of healthy girls who spend much time in the sun. She looked somewhat flushed with excitement. He saw her father glaring at him, a tough-looking little man with ram's-horn mustaches, shaggy brows, and the amber eyes of a mountain lion. The look meant nothing. He was stupid and completely inept. He actually sang hymns in the back room when he was worried!

"I wish you people would think about retiring and enjoying the good things," Hughson said. "My offer to buy you out still stands."

"Havin' troubles, are you?" old Daniel Reese leered.

Before Hughson could answer, Sylvester Morton was coming toward them. Hughson quickly stepped forward and offered his hand. At the same moment, Justina put herself in Morton's path. The postal inspector looked surprised and bewildered, glancing from one to the other. Then he smiled, shook hands with Hughson, nodded pleasantly to the girl.

"I have my turnout," Hughson said quickly. "Mrs. Hughson will be heartbroken if you don't dine with us—"

Justina laughed, a musical sound with throatiness in it. "Don't listen to him, Mr. Morton! Father and I regard your visits as the high points of our year. We'd be *so* pleased—"

Morton said, "Folks, you're all too kind, but I have a previous engagement. Besides, I leave at eleven o'clock."

"Brandy and cigars then, before you leave—" Hughson pressed him.

Morton bit his lip. "Well...all right. Ten o'clock?"

"Fine—at my office. I'll have you on the stage when it leaves."

Morton hurried into the stage office. The Reeses, disappointed, moved off.

Bracing himself, Hughson turned to look at the young fellow who had stood in the background all the while. Rian McCool was gazing steadily at him. He looked pallid but fit. Beside his mouth were two deep, bitter lines he did not remember. There was a change in the way he looked at a man, too—a cold intensification of a certain natural bluntness.

"Artie Judd sent his best," McCool remarked easily.

"His best," said Hughson calmly, "is none too good."

"Neither is mine," McCool replied. "Be sure you don't bring out the worst in me."

Hughson saw the gun in his holster. He could only speculate on what had taken place in Vallecito. Dead or alive, Judd had come off second best. What he knew, as surely as he knew anything, was that McCool had to be killed or bought off.

As McCool started to pass, Hughson spoke.

"What's your hurry? We'll only have to hunt each other up later and say what's on our minds."

He turned and walked into the stage station without a backward glance, and McCool started to follow. Then he halted, with a dark look of anger. The way men like Hughson—the takers of this world—made their moves with such high-chinned confidence. It galled him almost as much as the way his own kind, the natural-born givers, frisked along after them like lap dogs!

Yet Hughson was right. What was to be said might as well be said early as late. He followed him.

Hughson's office, behind the baggage room, contained an oak desk, some cabinets and a cuspidor, on a checkered linoleum floor. The stage man sat down and took a cigar from a box in a drawer. Frowning, he struck a match and puffed the cigar to life. While he did so, McCool stood by the door watching him.

Hughson blew smoke at the ceiling. "Now then," he said. "How did you get Artie's gun?"

"Aren't you going to ask me to sit down?" McCool grinned cynically.

Hughson waved his hand. "Get comfortable. I'm sorry."

"The hell you are. You're a damned poor actor. But I don't know how to fence either—or whatever they call it—so I'll just hack away with a blunt cleaver and see if I can get through to you. I got Judd's gun by being a little faster and a lot smarter than he is. I'm banking that I'm smarter than you are, too. And I'll bet I can sink my teeth deeper. I won't be easy to shake off."

Hughson rolled the cigar in his teeth.

"So maybe you'd better pay me what that ranch was worth," McCool suggested. "Then I'll leave you alone."

"What *was* it worth? Out of curiosity, I mean."

"Twenty-five hundred dollars."

The heavy lids of Hughson's eyes descended, then raised, and he regarded McCool through a somber mask of contempt. "What makes you think you've got that much nuisance value to me?"

"I'm selling land, not nuisance value. I'll knock off five hundred dollars," McCool said.

"For what?"

Rian grinned, his expression brash. It made Hughson think of a barefisted slugger coming off the ropes with a bloody face but a reckless glint in his eyes.

"For cash. Put two thousand dollars in my pocket and you'll never see me again."

"And if I don't?"

"Then," McCool told him, "you'll be so sick of seeing me a month from now that you'll pay three thousand."

Hughson tilted his face up and blew smoke at the ceiling. "No deal."

"So you're broke already."

"What makes you think so?"

"I told you I was smart, didn't I? I know as much about your business as you know yourself—maybe more. And I'm going to break you like a stick, and probably get your wife in the bargain."

He turned and opened the door, but lingered before going out. Hughson watched him, pondering. Something had happened to that fellow in jail. He'd gotten religion or something; had a kind of prideful confidence he'd never shown before. The change in him both alarmed and angered George Hughson. His glance dropped to the drawer, still open, from which he had taken the cigar. A bronze-framed Colt lay behind the cigar box. A rush of blood to his head dizzied him for a moment.

*Why not kill him?* he thought breathlessly. *All I would have to tell Marshal Fowley is: "The fool came charging in here yelling he was going to kill me!"*

His hand closed on the revolver, his eyes on the back of McCool's old blue jacket. But the shaggy red head turned abruptly and McCool was regarding him curiously. Hughson cautiously drew his hand from the drawer.

"You're a damned fool," he said. "You never broke anything but a horse in your life, and you won't break me. If you're still around town in the morning, you'll be asking for a fight in a ring where we wear brass knuckles and the bell's broken."

Rian smacked his fist against his palm. "Ah!" he said. "The kind of fight I like best."

"But probably not the kind of odds," retorted Hughson.

As soon as the door had closed behind McCool, Hughson left his desk and opened a door which gave onto the stage yard in the rear. Before the stage barn, a deep-chested man with the coarse build of a laborer, wearing brown suit pants and a clean shirt, was supervising the care of the coach and team.

He shouted at the Mexican hostlers who were handling the team. "If I catch you again turning a team in to roll without you cool it out first, I'll break your necks! That's the last time I aim to tell you."

"Biff," Hughson called quickly.

Biff Shackley, his superintendent, turned with a scowl. He was a crudely made man with an enormous chest and thick arms. His features were red and intemperate, but his gray hair was neatly cut and brushed. Without a word, he walked to the little porch behind Hughson's office.

"What's the matter?" he asked.

"There's a man just leaving the station," Hughson said. "Young fellow, about six feet, wearing a denim jacket. See him?"

Shackley's eyes quested through the group of passengers clotted around the street gate. "Yeah. Kind of red hair?" he muttered. "Say, is that—?" The big man's features sagged.

Hughson nodded. "Keep an eye on him, Biff. I want to see where he goes. Don't let him see you."

Shackley passed a hand over his hair, dazed. "But I thought Artie—"

"So did I," Hughson said drily. "That's Artie's gun in his holster. Don't ask me," he said sharply. "Follow him, then come back and *tell* me."

# Chapter Six

McCool HAD WALKED a hundred feet down the warm, dusty street, the sun slanting in deeply from the west, when he realized a man was blocking his path. He halted and threw a quick look at him. Immediately he saw the marshal's shield on his coat.

The man was tall, with a dry, hard-fleshed look, and he wore full sandy mustaches. He was dressed in a gray suit, dark tie with a loose knot, a cityish gray felt hat resting on the side of his head.

"What's your name?" he asked sharply.

McCool smiled. "Judd," he said. "Artie Judd."

The marshal looked him over carefully. "It's Judd's gun, all right," he said.

"The fact of the matter is," Rian told him. "I met

Judd in Vallecito and he asked me to bring his gun on for him. He said he'd be along later. What's *your* name?" he asked pleasantly.

"Marshal Fowley. I don't have a lot of use for Judd, but I don't need any smart-talking citizens like you either. I'm asking once more what your name is. Then I'll take you in for questioning."

"Rian McCool."

"How did you get the gun, McCool?"

"Artie pulled it on me," Rian said frankly. "One thing led to another and—well, he decided to rest up before he came back. He'll be along tomorrow, more than likely. Say, is there a good, cheap hotel in this town?" he asked.

"There's a good one, and there's a cheap one. Judging by the cut of your clothes, I think you might like the cheap one better. It's the Frontera Hotel. What's your business in town?"

"I'm not sure yet. I'll look into the prospects and invest where it looks like I'd get the best return."

Marshal Fowley's wide jaws bulged a little as the muscles worked. He said, "I'll probably see you later," and passed on.

Rian walked another fifty feet, glanced back, and saw him enter the stage station.

At the Frontera Hotel, he took a dollar-fifty room. It was a sort of kennel under an outside stairway, with a door to the hotel backhouse and an inside door on a dingy hallway. It was furnished with a sour-smelling cot, a granite-ware washpan, and a baking powder can full of soft soap.

He lay down for a moment, resting his arm across his eyes.

His thoughts swung to Morton. Would he ever see him again? Ever see his fifty bucks? Somehow it did not seem to matter whether Morton was an artful con man or not. What he had spoken was the truth. And that, by God, was that you were as good as you made people think you were. He had noticed a sort of flinching in the eyes of George Hughson just now. It did not mean that he would back off, but it signified that he saw a change in him.

What Morton had sold him for fifty dollars was the knowledge that the thing to do with your hat was not to tip it to everybody, but to cock it over your eyes and barge right in.

He slept for a few minutes. Waking, he found himself thinking of the marshal. No question but what Fowley would come to him eventually and take the gun away from him. He would have to surrender it or go to war with the law. Scratching his shaggy head, he sat on the edge of the cot and held the revolver in his hands. His mouth slowly broke into a grin. He flipped out the loading gate, punched the heavy cartridges onto the cot, then examined the gun hammer. He shoved the gun under the pillow and left the room.

He returned in ten minutes with a fifty-cent whetstone. He took off a sixteenth of an inch. When he was finished, the hammer looked about the same, but the firing pin was too short to reach the cap. The gun would not fire. Unless Judd, who knew his weapon as a man knew his wife's lips, noticed the change and had a new firing pin installed.

Still, it was worth trying.

Marshal Fowley was in his office when Rian

walked in a few minutes later. He was going through some old warrants. Seeing Rian, he started and quickly shoved the whole batch into a drawer. *He's looking for something on me*, thought Rian.

He laid the Colt on Fowley's desk, smiling wryly. "Why fight it?" he said. "It's Judd's gun. I don't think it's very lucky anyhow. Give it to him with my regards."

Fowley smiled and picked the gun up. He hefted it, then dropped it in a drawer. "McCool, you've got a good head. A much better one than I was just hearing from an old friend of yours."

"Hughson? What'd he tell you?"

"I don't discuss such business. But I'll say this: a man that's done his time and behaves himself, draws the same amount of water in my town as a man that's never been in trouble."

"I'll shake on that, Marshal," said Rian.

They shook hands and he left.

According to the hotel clerk, the office of the Empire Stage Lines—Hughson's competitor—was on an intersecting street a block south of the center of town. Rian was strolling in that direction when he saw a young woman come from a store building and start down the walk.

She moved with short strides, and there was a vitality about the brisk sway of her skirts that brought him fully awake. He recognized her by her reddish-gold hair: Justina Reese.

Rian stepped up his stride, and just before he caught her she glanced around to see who was following. Then she looked straight ahead, continued on to the corner, and turned right.

Rian followed. She glanced at him again as he caught up. When he did not pass her, she slowed down. Rian slowed, too. She gave him a quick stare of vexation and he smiled. She was remarkably attractive, her features delicately cast but without any Dresden-china look about them. She took his measure frankly, then stopped.

When Rian stopped also, she spoke calmly. "I can raise my voice, mister, and ten men will be beating you in half a minute," she said.

Rian removed his hat. "Yes, ma'am, but then you wouldn't get to meet the man that's going to knock George Hughson into a cocked hat. And that'd be a shame, wouldn't it?"

Justina frowned, started to speak, then bit her lip and hesitated. "Who are you?" she asked.

Rian glanced around, then handed her Morton's business card.

"My name's McCool. But let's think of me as a friend of Sylvester Morton's instead of plain old Rian McCool."

The girl read the card and the message on its reverse side. Then she gave him a smile which caused his flesh to crawl. It flashed intimacy, eagerness and admiration. "Any friend of Mr. Morton's," she said enthusiastically, "is certainly a friend of Father's and mine. We'll be having dinner in just a few minutes. Won't you join us?"

"You'd better believe I will," Rian said with a grin.

# Chapter Seven

THERE WAS A small stage depot on a corner, a gate to a stage yard behind it, and half the number of corrals a going stage line needed for its main terminus. Under a shelter was a single coach, an old Concord wagon. Not a hostler was in sight.

All the brass and nickel brightwork Rian discerned was dull; the harness hanging on wall pegs cried out for saddle soap. As they walked to a small, flat-roofed adobe building at the rear of the yard, he picked up two or three stones and a chunk of black iron lopped off a horseshoe when the shoer fitted a horse.

Justina gazed at him uneasily. "What is it? Are you collecting ammunition for a slingshot, Mr. McCool?"

"No, ma'am. But I'm a horseman, and I hate to think of a horse getting any of this trash lodged in a frog of its hoof."

"Oh," the girl said.

The building at the rear was the Reese's small home. A wonderful fragrance of home-cooked food filled it. After a year of jail cooking Rian almost broke down. He met the amber-eyed, tough-looking little man he had seen with Justina at the stage station: Dan Reese, her father.

Shaking hands with Reese was somehow puzzling. He had the grim face and leathery look of a retired town-tamer. But his grip was pulpy, and his eyes shied from direct contact. When you confronted him, you felt his diffidence and knew you were shaking hands with a dreamer. Just the sort of man George Hughson ate raw, without seasoning.

Old Dan Reese poured elderberry wine for McCool, who drank it thinking it would have been just right on pancakes, while he yearned for the bite of whiskey. They ate, Justina chatering brightly and Rian trying to decide how a man put pressure on people like these. But only pressure would buy him the percentage of their company, which he needed.

"Tell us about Mr. Morton," Justina murmured as they got settled in the parlor after dinner. "He seems *such* a nice man."

Rian nodded. "They don't come better than Sylvester."

"And what is your business, Mr. McCool?" asked the girl.

"I'm a stage man," Rian said, nodding and trying to believe it.

"Oh?" The girl and her father exchanged glances, puzzled. She gave a little laugh. "I hope you aren't going into competition with us?"

"No, no! The truth of the matter is, I'm thinking of buying with an existing stage line."

"But—but you said something about tangling with Mr. Hughson."

"Yes. There isn't room for three lines. Morton thinks there isn't actually room for two. I told him what was on my mind, and he said, 'Talk to George Hughson and Dan Reese. One of them might be willing to sell you an interest.' But I know Hughson and I don't like him. So I thought I'd talk to you."

"Well, well," the girl said after a moment.

Dan Reese cleared his throat. "How much money do you have to invest?" he asked in his furry old-man's voice.

"Not much. But I know staging, I'm ambitious, and I don't mind hard work."

Justina smiled with the expression of a woman who feared to hurt someone's feelings. "Perhaps," she said, "What you're looking for is a job rather than a partner, Mr. McCool."

Rian's snub features crinkled with good humor. "No," he said, "I've held jobs, as well as running my own outfit, and you can take it from me there's no future in jobs. So I thought I'd put it to you just that way: I'll pull this stage line out of the red and practically guarantee you'll get your mail contract renewed. All it'll cost you is one-third interest. And I'll throw in a note for $1,000, payable six months after we get that renewal."

"You must be joking!" Dan Reese said. "Why,

I've got thousands in this line!"

Leaning forward, Rian rested his elbows on his knees and linked his fingers. "I know. But how much is the line *worth*? Considering that you're losing money, and about to lose your mail contract?"

Justina gasped. "How do you know that?"

"Just surmising from things I've heard. It doesn't seem to me like a line that's in debt up to its hocks is worth much more than I'm offering."

The girl sat up straight, her clear, calm features weighing it. "No," she said. "It isn't. If we lose that contract, it isn't worth anything. We owe so much—and so many people owe us—that we wouldn't survive a month."

Rian's eyebrows raised. "There's money owed you?"

"Heavens, yes! Potter's Feed owes over six hundred dollars for *higar* cane we've hauled in our freight wagons."

"I didn't see any freight wagons," McCool said, frowning.

The Reeses glanced at each other.

"There was a slide on the Johnson grade," Justina murmured. "The wagons were—well, we hope to have them back in shape soon."

"Who's your superintendent?"

"A man named Brogan. But he's stationed in Frontera, at the other end of the line."

Rian shook his head. "A super should live on the premises. I don't know," he sighed. "Maybe this outfit is past saving."

"Oh, no! It's really not so bad as that. And a man

like yourself who understands business practices and all—who knows, perhaps we could have it running like a top in no time." She smiled dazzlingly.

*My God!* Rian thought. *Now* she's *selling the idea to* me!

Prowling to the door, he gazed out on the stage yard. He kicked the screen door open to see better. It was growing dark now. He squinted. A man on the sidewalk was standing beside the station. Perhaps he did not know he was visible; a night light in the office silhouetted his bearish profile.

Biff Schackley! Not a question in the world! One of the men who had put him in jail for a year and stripped the hide off him.

Rian tingled as he turned back. "I'll tell you what. Out of fairness to both parties, I think I ought to take the books to my hotel room and look them over. See whether I think I can help. Find out who owes you how much, all that kind of thing. I'll bring them back in the morning. If we're all in agreement, we'll have some papers drawn up."

Justina bit her lip. Her father said, "Now see here—" but the girl rose and came toward Rian. She peered into his eyes. Then she gave a soft laugh.

"It's insane!" she said. "I wouldn't be surprised if you've never so much as dusted off a stagecoach in your life."

Rian grinned. "I've dusted off a few men though, Miss Justina. And that's your real problem, isn't it?"

She did not answer. "Father and I will talk it over. You may take the books with you. Unless we come to our senses overnight, we'll probably cut you in for your outrageous third interest."

He put out his hand. She gave him hers, slender and nervous-feeling, then quickly drew it away. Rian turned and shook hands with Dan Reese. The old man began telling him about some of their troubles with wagons and stages rolling off grades. He sounded plaintive and confused.

"How are you going to fight people like that?" he asked. "The law's no help. And I'm too old to deal with the scoundrels myself."

Rian patted his shoulder. "I'm not too old, Dan," he said. "I'm just the right age. That reminds me—you wouldn't have an old hogleg you could spare for a few days, would you? I came here without so much as a blowgun."

"Sure would!"

Dan Reese left the room. Rian heard him opening and closing drawers. After a few minutes he returned. "Swore I left it in my dresser," he said. "I'll find it tomorrow and loan it to you."

"That's all right."

Rian and the girl walked from the house to the stage office. Justina went in and came out carrying a heavy ledger. Rian took the book from her hands. The moment was dark and intimate. She smiled and looked down.

Then, around the corner of the building, he heard a man clear his throat. He listened, but the girl seemed not to have heard the sound.

"I'm afraid there's more bad news than good in the book," she said. "But do read it and tell us what you think. Good night now."

He watched her return to the house. She walked a

little more briskly than before, he thought. He pictured the scene in the parlor as they discussed him: con man or savior? The more he thought about it, the more he believed he would earn his money around this yard. Starting now.

He opened the latch of the gate, moved through, and turned to close it. Ten feet away, in the alcoved rectangle of the depot's door, he made out the shape of a man standing in the shadows.

Normally, a man would turn left from the gate and head toward the main street. Probably that was what Biff Shackley had counted on. Whistling, Rian turned right and moved along close to the wall of the station, approaching Shackley. The superintendent pressed back, trying to keep out of sight.

*You're a hell of a tracker*, thought Rian. He could actually smell the man—whiskey, sweat, and some kind of sweet toilet water.

As he came abreast of Shackley, he groped in his pocket for a match. Then, feigning surprise at the big man's presence, he said, "Say, friend—hold this book a minute, will you?"

He thrust the big volume against Shackley's belly. Shackley automatically put his hands under it, as though to carry a baby. Rian turned calmly, cocked his fist, and drove clean and hard to his chin.

Shackley groaned as his head collided with the door. Rian hit him again. Quickly he caught the book as the superintendent dropped it. Shackley fell to his knees, making coughing sounds, blundering forward in an attempt to catch Rian around the knees. Rian drove his knee into Shackley's face. The man sprawled sideways across the walk.

Rian set the book down and hauled Shackley to his feet, staggering. He was surprised at his bulk. He was a big man, no mistake. But he was hurt, and Rian jammed him against the wall, held him with one hand, and cocked his right.

"What's the matter, Biff? Horses knock all your brains out?" he growled.

Shackley's eyes were half closed; his nose was streaming blood. He raised a hand limply and pawed at Rian's shoulder.

"Compliments of the Vallecito jail," Rian said. "What *was* going on in the office that night?"

Shackley made a tongueless muttering.

"There was kerosene burning, wasn't there?" Rian said. "A pan of kerosene. I've thought about it for a year, and that's all I know that would burn blue and yellow. How come? Were you burning the place down for the insurance?"

Suddenly Shackley gathered himself and shoved him away. He came at him with a slow, loose swing. Rian went under the blow and smashed back at the super's face. His knuckles bit through Shackley's lips. Shackley stumbled aside, clutched at the wall, and went down again.

Rian took his gun and tossed it into a horse trough. Then he picked up the ledger, rolled Shackley's head with his foot, and said:

"Night, old buddy. Come see me at the Frontera. That's where I'm staying, if that's what the boss man sent you to find out."

In his room Rian washed up and found he had stripped some hide off his knuckles. Shackley would be out of his mind with rage. He was a muscular bull of a man, and even considered himself rather sly. And he'd been suckered into a trap like that!

Smiling to himself, Rian sat down to look at the books of the Empire Stage Company. Before he started, he looked at his watch. Eight-thirty. Two hours till his date with Sylvester Morton at the Pastime Bar.

# Chapter Eight

AT NINE O'CLOCK, George Hughson heard the door of Biff Shackley's room creak open. Quickly, Hughson rolled to his feet and started out the side door to hurry to the superintendent's room at the end of the long stage building. He had been waiting an hour, wondering what had happened, and chewing on his visit with Rian McCool.

"I know as much about your business as you do!" the fool had bragged. It was a lie, of course. But what had put that particular lie into his mouth?

Hughson remembered seeing McCool talking with Sylvester Morton, the postal inspector. Any connection there? His mind handled all these factors restlessly and without satisfaction. Something was going on, and he must know what it was damned soon. He was relieved that Shackley had finally come back.

Hughson's muscular body slipped through the door into the yard. He turned left and strode along the wall to the rear of the building. As he passed the super's window, he saw a lamp flare up behind the grimy panes. The door was still open. He hit the doorjamb with his boot, in lieu of knocking, and moved inside.

The room, dimly lighted by a wall lamp, smelled of liniment, whiskey, and sweat—a hard-living bachelor's bedroom, festooned with cobwebs in all the corners. On the scarred dresser were arrayed bottles of every kind—liquor, hair tonic, patent medicines. Shackley was bent over a washbowl on the commode.

"What kept you?" Hughson asked.

Shackley grunted something unintelligible. He scooped water up in his hands, buried his face in it, and snorted so that the spray flew. Hughson's eyes suddenly narrowed. He walked up behind Shackley and turned him angrily.

"Have you been boozing it up?" he demanded.

Then he caught his breath. Shackley's mouth was swollen as though wild bees had stung it. One eye was puffed. Tears of rage brimmed in his whiskey-fighter's eyes.

"So help me—!" he choked.

"What happened?" Hughson reached for a bottle on the dresser. He drew the cork from a pint of Mountain Brook and put it in Shackley's hands.

Shackley drank deeply. Then he sat on the edge

of his cot and told the story. His words were garbled
by his puffed lips. He stopped twice and took some
more whiskey.

"What kind of book?" Hughson muttered.

"A ledger," Shackley said.

"A *ledger?* Why?"

Shackley shook his head. "I heard the girl say
something about 'bad news' in the book, but he
could look it over and tell them what he thought—"

With a machinelike click, facts began snapping
into place in the stage man's mind. He was shocked,
first; then filled with a kind of joyful rage.

"That stupid jailbird!" he said. "He's planning to
buy in with Dan Reese. How do you like that, Biff?
He's going into competition with me!"

Shackley did not seem to know or care what he
was saying. From pegs beside the door, he lifted
down an old revolving carbine. He sat on the bed
and used an oiled rag to dust it. He breathed loudly
through his nose. Hughson reached down and took
the rifle from his hands.

When Shackley rose, a frown of anger in his eyes,
Hughson smiled: "Not so fast, Biff. We'll serve him
with an apple in his mouth, but not that way. We
don't need to get ourselves hung, do we?"

Shackley reached for the gun again, and
Hughson put it behind him, chuckling.

"I like your spirit, Biff, even if you don't show
much brains sometimes. Now listen. He's got a date
with Morton at the Pastime tonight. I'll try to work
things so that he leaves by the back door. I want you
to pick up Spence and a couple of men you can

count on, and be in the alley to meet him. Take him out of town and give him a working over he won't forget."

It was getting through to Shackley now. Dabbing at a cut on his face with a towel, he growled, "He won't come back. By God, he won't!"

Hughson smiled grimly. "Don't get carried away."

The shaggy head shook. "Say, I remember him saying something else. I was laying there and I felt him take my gun out of the holster. He said something about kerosene—"

Hughson cocked one eye. "Kerosene?"

"—something about it burning blue and yellow. And he said—lemme think—he said, 'What was going on in that stage station, Biff?'"

George Hughson turned and replaced the gun on the wall pegs. Without looking at Shackley again, he said, "Now I *know* he's not coming back. Take care of him."

As he went out, he heard Shackley say, "I know just the thing. Cactus..."


At ten o'clock, Hughson drifted into the Pastime Bar. He found Morton in a card game. The little postal inspector sat rigidly on the edge of his chair, bucking the house in a game of blackjack. His black derby rested on the back of his head and a thin film of perspiration glistened on his skin.

Hughson saw that there were very few chips in front of Morton. He watched the inspector's fingers drum on the green cloth; he peered keenly into the tormented face and recognized at once the weakness he had always suspected in the man.

He had the gambling fever.

Morton had sixteen points showing now, and the dealer was waiting for him to decide whether to stand pat or try another card.

"Hit me," Morton said, and then bit his lip in swift remorse.

A ten landed atop his cards.

He was out.

He pushed his last few chips onto the table and Hughson watched him draw twenty and sit there cracking his knuckles, while the dealer turned up fifteen and dealt himself a six.

Twenty-one.

Morton's chips were swept away.

Morton got up. He was shuffling toward the bar when Hughson tapped his arm.

"Hello," he said cheerfully.

Morton gazed at him, his eyes vacant. "We had a date for a drink, remember?" Hughson said.

The inspector recovered. "Oh, sure. Sorry. Got a lot of things on my mind. Yes, I'll have a brandy."

After three brandies, Morton confided, "A half-hour ago I was two hundred dollars ahead. If I'd had another fifty, I'd've beat the house. You've got to have a bank roll. You can't do it on peanuts."

Hughson drew some coins from his pocket. He placed four double eagles and two gold eagles on the bar. "If you've got a blank check on you," he said, "you can still go back and make that tiger howl."

Morton stared at the money, then groped in his pocket until he found a wrinkled checkbook. He wrote a check for a hundred dollars, gripped the stage man's hand briefly, and rushed away with the money.

Hughson had a second brandy and looked at the clock. Ten-fifteen. With the fever on him heavy, Morton would probably lose the hundred in a few minutes. Especially when primed with brandy. But still it was cutting it close. McCool was due in fifteen minutes.

Before long the little man in the black suit came drifting back. He accepted without a word the fourth drink Hughson offered, staring at the back-bar as though he had just crawled from the wreckage of a stage which had gone over a bank.

Laying the check on the bar, Hughson said thoughtfully, "I suppose I might as well get the saloon to cash this for me now—"

Morton started. Then he gripped his wrist. "No! That is—it's up to you, of course, but—well, I'd appreciate it if you could give me a couple of days to cover it."

Hughson looked into his face sternly. "About how long?"

"Two weeks be all right?"

Hughson relaxed, patting the man's arm and chuckling. "A month, if you say so, Sylvester. You can make it up to me sometime."

Morton clasped his hand with drunken affection. "You're all right, George. You're okay. You bet I will."

Then his expression changed. He was staring toward the front. Hughson glanced around and saw Rian McCool standing near the entrance, that same cocksure half-smile on his face as he searched the saloon for Morton. Suddenly McCool was staring at Morton. He started through the crowd toward them.

Leaning toward Morton, Hughson murmured, "Excuse me, but you look a little ill, Mr. Morton. The outhouses are through that door, on the alley."

Morton gulped and nodded. "Thanks! I'll see you next time."

He hurried out the back door into the alley.

In the mirror, Hughson watched McCool come on. The big redhead stopped and stared at his back. The stage man stood tensely. Then McCool hurried up, opened the door, and followed Morton into the alley.

## Chapter Nine

RIAN STEPPED INTO the middle of the alley and peered through the darkness. He saw a row of outhouses across the rutted, weed-flanked alley. Wood smoke was in the air; the smell of the stage stable, a short distance up the line, came to him. There were dark glints from heaps of empty bottles. A pyramid of kegs stood against the back of the saloon building.

But there was no sign of Sylvester Morton. *The little grease ant*, Rian thought with a grin. *Maybe the whole thing was just Morton's way of setting me up for a fifty-dollar touch.*

He laughed softly and shook his head. *If it was, he's sure turned a tiger loose in the streets with his crackerbarrel philosophizing! Started a war, maybe.*

Gravel made a crisp sound near him, and his head turned. A man was standing beside the beer kegs ranked against the wall.

"Morton—?" he called uncertainly.

Then there was hissing indraw of breath behind him and he flung an arm up for protection and dodged away. The man beside the wall stepped into his path, raising a short length of iron bar. Rian threw a fist at his face and felt a satisfying crunch of meat and bone. But the bar came down on his shoulder and he groaned and staggered into the alley.

Another man tackled him behind the knees. As he fell, someone else—he could see a bandanna mask on the man's face—stepped in close and hammered at Rian's head with his fists. Two blows hit solidly. A cold blackness engulfed him. He lay still, hoping for a moment to clear his head. A rancid perfume of perspiration and toilet water reached his nostrils. Shackley!

The man with the bar loomed over him; Rian's guts clutched in terror and he tried to roll away. A booted foot stopped him with a kick in the ribs. A man muttered, "Hold on—you'll kill him!"

But almost immediately a blow landed on Rian's head, and a bright splash of pain exploded inside his skull.

The next thing he knew was that he was being hauled along the alley, his toes dragging. His head hung loosely. A thought blew through his head like an old paper bag down an alley. *Dan Reese, you old idiot! If you'd remembered where you kept that gun, maybe you'd still have a partner . . .*

A wagon with two horses on the doubletree waited behind the stage yard. They lifted him onto the bed, wrenched his arms up behind him and tied his wrists together. With a sob of desperation he drew his knees up and kicked his boots straight out. Someone swore and fell off the wagon. He squirmed into a sitting position.

A club hit his head with a solid smack.

"Is there a man named McCool—Rian McCool—staying here?" Justina asked the desk clerk at the Frontera Hotel. She was carrying the biggest handbag she owned, a tapestry bag in the bottom of which lay her father's revolver. In the last drawer in the house, after looking everywhere, Dan had found it.

"Yes. He went out about ten-fifteen, though," said the clerk.

The girl hesitated. Then she smiled. "Well, thank you."

On the sidewalk, she stood undecided whether to look any farther. He must have felt he needed the gun or he would be in some saloon, and she certainly was not going to prowl around town looking through saloon windows.

She walked back to her corner and turned west toward the depot. Just before she reached it, a wagon rattled out of the intersecting street. There was enough light so that she could make out the yellow and green colors of the Hughson line on its sideboards. She wrinkled her nose in distaste.

Reaching the gate, she started to turn in. Then she saw something odd.

A man was lying on the bed of the wagon! Two men were on the seat, and a couple of others were riding backwards on the tail gate. The man driving, hunched over like a bear, was too large to be anyone but Biff Shackley.

In her breast, anxiety began to flutter like a moth in a lamp chimney. Was that Mr. McCool lying in the wagon? She knew Hughson and his superintendent were completely ruthless. Could they have gotten wind of the proposed partnership? The wagon rattled on down the dark street until it was out of sight. Justina hurried across the stage yard to the house.

"Father!" she called as she ran in.

He was gone. His hat was not on the antelope prong where he always kept it. She remembered now that he had spoken of going to the hotel to play dominoes with some of his cronies. She thought of the marshal. But by the time she got back with him the wagon would be long gone.

Justina hurried to the corral and took a bridle from a peg. She walked in among the horses and spoke the name of her saddle horse. The little buckskin mare stood passively while she pushed the bit into her mouth and pulled the crown strap over her ears. After leading the horse out, Justina lifted her side saddle onto its back and made the cinches tight. She was hardly dressed for riding, but it was no time to fret about the proprieties.

She drew the pistol from her handbag and, not finding a suitable place to carry it, unfastened two buttons of her gown and thrust it into the bodice.

As she rode down the street, she thought, *What*

*in the world am I doing? Have I lost my mind? He
isn't even a partner yet—nor a friend! Just a strange,
likable young man who's dropped into my life like
an unexpected gift.*

She flicked the horse with the reins and it jogged
faster.

The white paring of moon above the hills shed a
faint light in the wash where the wagon was parked.
Rian was conscious now, a raw, pulsing pain in his
skull. They had spread-eagled him to a wheel of the
wagon, facing it, ankles and wrists lashed to the rim.

Shackley caught him by the hair and yanked his
head around. Thrusting his face close, he said,
"How do you like this kind of party, scrapper?"

McCool spat in his face.

Shackley rammed his head against the spokes
and cursed him. "Dirty, ignorant horse-buster!" he
shouted. He turned and yelled into the darkness.
"Spence—what're you doing?"

Spence called something from the dry jungle of
sage and cactus stretching away from the bank of
the wash. Presently he came back and jumped down
to the sand.

Rian looked at him, wanting to remember him
clearly. All the men had pulled down their
bandanna masks after they'd left town. He was
small and lithe, with hard eyes, bony features and a
gopherish mouth. He was carrying a couple of
ocotillo wands—branches from the cactus, sometimes called "wolf candle." He squatted down and
began cutting away from one end the wicked
fishhooklike thorns with a pair of wire cutters. Each

wand was about four feet long.

"These do it?" he asked Shackley.

Rian's eyes squeezed out. A silent scream echoed through his whole being. The Comanche treatment: a whipping with cactus wands. There was natural poison on every thorn.

Shackley pulled on heavy gloves while Spence prepared the whips. He backhanded Rian across the mouth. "You don't like this kind of *baile*, do you?" he said. "You just like to step up and mash a man in the face without warning."

"Without warning's the way you mashed me that night," Rian said.

"You were drunk. What the hell do you know about it?"

"I know something was going on in there. I know something else, too, Biff. If you lay that whip to my back, I'll kill you for it. I'll live that long, unless you kill me outright."

Shackley chuckled. "Am I shaking?" he asked the other men, holding out his gloved hands.

"You're in terrible shape," said the wolfish little man named Spence. "Here—how's this?"

Shackley took the trimmed whip in his gloved hand. He handled it carefully, respectful of the thorns. Then he took a sudden cut at Rian's back, hitting the wagon instead. Rian made a hoarse cry of terror. Shackley went into a windy convulsion of laughter.

"Oh, my God!" he said. "This is going to be better than a horse-gelding."

He set himself, working his boots into the sand. Spence raised his hand.

"Wait a minute, Biff. Hear that?"

"Yes, I hear it. We're only a mile from the county road. It's a buckboard going by."

His eyes closed tight, Rian heard Shackley's grunt of exertion, then a whistle in the air; then he felt a pain so great that his whole body leaped as the whip seared his shoulder and back. The horses snorted and danced forward a few feet. The wheel to which he was tied revolved a quarter turn, so that he was left lying parallel to the ground.

"Back 'em up, back 'em up," the super muttered. "Can't lash a man in that position."

Two of the other men backed the horses until the figure cross-tied to the wheel was back in position. Rian felt blood running down his back. Shackley swung the whip again. The terrible pain of a hundred thorn punctures brought another scream from Rian's lips. He could feel both strokes like strips burned in his flesh by a branding iron. In dumb animal agony, he sobbed aloud.

Shackley came up and twisted his head around. "Is that the kind of *baile* you favor, scrapper?" he asked. "Because I ain't tired yet."

Biting his lip, Rian clenched the wagon spokes with both hands. The pain was spreading, scalding his entire back.

"You see, we been trying to tell you something," Shackley was saying. "We want you to go to some other town that you might like better. Any old town. Just so it's clear away from here. So when we turn you loose tonight, don't you even think of coming back."

"I guess about a dozen more ought to do it," Shackley said.

Once more he set himself. Then the wash was

illuminated by a flash and roar that dazzled the eyes and made the ears ring. Even with his eyes closed, Rian was blinded. He heard the men bawling questions at each other. Then there was a second crashing explosion bursting out of a core of yellow fire, and one of the group screamed. Rian twisted his head. He saw Shackley fire a wild shot into the brush lining the arroyo, then cut and run. He saw a man lying on the sand.

In the same instant, the wagon team began to run. Rian clung to the spokes, shouting, "Ho! Ho, now!" But the horses kept running. He was spinning slowly on the wheel. The wagon wheels, deeply bogged in sand, kept the animals from running fast. But Rian, from pain and the blood in his head, soon lost consciousness.

# Chapter Ten

WHEN HE CAME to his senses, he was lying face down on the wagon as it went banging along over a graded road. He groaned.

A girl's voice said, "I'm sorry we have to have to go so fast, Mr. McCool! I think they're all afoot, but we can't take a chance of their catching us."

Huddling on his side on the wagon bed, he gritted his teeth against the pain. In a few minutes the wagon slowed; he looked up and saw buildings. He was in too much pain to wonder about anything when Justina Reese came around to help him from the wagon. With assistance, he was able to walk into the house and lie on the floor.

Before she commenced working, she brought him a bottle of black medicine resembling a strong purgative. "Drink some of this, Mr. McCool," she said. "It's Mother Winslow's Soothing Syrup—wonderful for pain."

He was willing to do anything that would blunt the edge of his pain. He drank heartily, and in a short time the most marvelous fuzziness invaded his brain, and he sighed deeply. The stuff was probably loaded with opium, he surmised. He took another gulp and settled down to making himself comfortable on the floor, curled up like a child.

"That's right, she murmured. "Go to sleep if you can."

Working carefully, she cut his shirt away and washed him to the waist, then treated the masses of small blue punctures with antiseptic. During most of the operation, he was in a restless sleep. Then he heard her father come in and exclaim in surprise.

Justina said reproachfully, "I thought you were going to play dominoes all night! Father, I—I killed a man!"

Dan Reese sat in a chair and stared at Rian. "No, he's still breathing," he said.

"I don't mean Mr. McCool!" She recounted the story. "So if there's an inquest," she concluded, "I'll just say it was self-defense."

"Don't say anything," Rian mumbled.

"What?"

"Don't tell them a thing," he said thickly. "It's their problem. Get me back to the hotel. Back door. Nobody'll see me."

"But, Mr. McCool—"

"Coffee," he muttered.

In some recess of his mind the thought was

lodged that he might be bad luck for the Reeses. Better if he were in his own room.

He loaded up on coffee. Between the hot drink and Mother Winslow's gentle ministrations, he felt relaxed and capable. Nevertheless, it required both of them to help him down the alley to the hotel. Dan Reese unlocked the outside door with Rian's key. Then he put his old Colt .45 in his holster. The two Reeses staggered into the room with him and stretched him out on the bed.

"What a horrible little room!" Justina gasped. "It smells like a mouse nest. Mr. McCool, I'll put this soothing syrup right here where you can reach it. Tomorrow I'll bring some more, in case you need it."

"I'll need it," Rian muttered.

"Do you think I killed that man?" the girl whispered.

"I hope so," Rian said. "Good night. Did you leave the gun?"

Dan Reese shoved it under his pillow. "It's loaded," he warned.

Rian's laugh was a croak of delirium. "I hope to hell it's loaded!" he said.

When he awoke, it seemed to be daylight. But he saw the little forked tongue of the lamp trembling inside the sooty lamp chimney on the dresser and decided it was still night.

He reached under the pillow to check on the gun. Hot little pustules erupted in pain the length of his back; he cried out and stifled the yell in the pillow. Eyes shut, he sent his hand groping along the floor for Mother Winslow. He found the bottle and took a swallow, spilling much of it on the cotton flannel sheet. Then he set the bottle down, groaning, and waited.

Relief came. He thought of Biff Shackley. *I'm going to live, Biff*, he thought. *But you aren't.*

Time telescoped.

Once, when he was awake, he recalled having eaten a meal. Who had fed him? Someone had made him sit on the edge of the bed and spooned food into his mouth. Justina? He vaguely remembered seeing reddish-gold hair in the lamplight. He had said something about it, in his foolish delirium and weakness. The girl had smiled, touched her hair, and thanked him.

At last, when he could get out of bed, he pulled on some pants and moved about the tiny floor. He could take five short strides, the long way. His chest was bandaged with torn sheets, and he could smell liniment. He felt stronger and very hungry.

Someone tapped on the door.

"Rian? Rian, dear, are you there?" a young woman called.

*Dear?* he thought. My goodness, what had he been saying to her? Someone must be putting something in my opium, he reflected. He opened the door.

Abby Hughson stood there in the hall.

Dark-haired and dainty, she reached her hand toward him timidly. Her eyes filled with tears as she looked at him. "Forgive me!"

A wicked content purred in Rian. "What for? You didn't do it."

76

"I did something worse. May I come in?"

Gesturing, he moved aside. She came into the room and closed the door. Impulsively, she came to him and pressed her cheek against his naked chest. "I'm so sorry—so ashamed!"

"Forget it," he said. He could see himself in the cracked mirror. His face was pale, his hair dark-red and ragged; her black hair against the whiteness of his chest stirred him. Once he would have given all he owned to have her in his arms. Now he thought: *Your time's coming, sister. It's coming.*

She roused to inspect his bandages. "Heavens, your bandages are *much* too tight! Who's your doctor?"

"Dr. Winslow."

"Winslow? He must be new; I don't know him. But wounds like that shouldn't have liniment on them, and they're bound too tightly to breathe. Lie down and let me fix them."

He lay on the bed, enjoying a sensuous comfort. She clucked like a mother hen.

"Pete's sake," he muttered, "I'm not going to die."

"You are," she said, "if you don't leave town. Artie Judd's back and waiting for you to show up. He's threatened to kill you. And Biff Shackley has been perfectly wild ever since the night you were hurt."

"Guess they'll have to take their chances with me."

"Aren't you going to leave?"

"I got one of George's men, didn't I? And I made a fool out of Artie. What makes them so sure they'll do any better the next time around?"

"Because they were only trying to scare you, up to now."

"And now you're trying?"

"Of course not."

"Then why are you here? To change my bandages?"

"To say how terribly sorry I am for the way I behaved in Vallecito," she murmured. "I was so confused—so unhappy—"

"How are things working out with old George?" he asked.

Abby sat up straight on the chair she had drawn to his bedside. "I'm afraid old George has all he wanted from me. My little bit of property."

"Then divorce him," Rian said. "Maybe we'll have another go at it, huh?"

"I know you're being bitter, but my answer would be yes, if you ever asked me again. But you see, I can't divorce him, because according to state law he owns everything that used to be mine!

"A rough law to buck," Rian admitted. He was astounded at how cold and deep she ran. But he was a full jump ahead of her, and waiting.

"Of course, when he dies—unless I predecease him—the property would be mine..."

"I s'pose," Rian said.

Abby finished dressing the wounds. She tossed the old bandages into the hall. Then she washed her hands, dried them daintily, and stood before him as he sat on the edge of the bed.

"I don't want anything to happen to you, Rian," she said. "Won't you go away, at least for a while?"

78

He smiled sadly. "I don't know what I'll do, Abby. I'm mad enough to kill all of them. But of course I'm not big enough."

"Maybe you are—with a little help," the girl said, smiling enigmatically.

"Now what's that mean?"

She tweaked his nose. "I'll tell you sometime. Right now, you just think about keeping out of sight and getting better."

As she was about to leave, she remembered something and pulled a pint bottle of whiskey from her handbag. With a smile, she set it on the dresser. "In case you need cheering up," she said.

"Thanks."

The door closed behind her.

*I'll be damned!* he thought. *She was asking me to kill him!*

*"Kill my husband, and you can have me!"*

He sat there, bemused. After a while he took a drink and painfully lay down to think about it.

# Chapter Eleven

THAT NIGHT, WHEN Justina visited him, she brought him a tray of good, solid food. It was not restaurant chow; she had cooked it herself. He put the tray on the chair and sat on the cot to eat. Justina glanced around, making a womanly check of things. Her roaming glance stopped abruptly. He felt a charge go through the room.

"You've been out," she said.

"No."

"Then where did the bottle of whiskey come from?"

Rian swallowed a mouthful of mashed potatoes. "Somebody brought it to me."

"I didn't know you were receiving visitors," Justina said.

Women definitely possessed senses a man didn't, he reflected—something like the olfactory organs of foxes, perhaps. She knew another woman had been in the room.

"Somebody came by to say hello," he told her.

"Oh."

After he ate, she made him lie down while she examined his bandages. "*What* in the *world*!" she exclaimed. "You've changed these. They're too loose. And you've sprinkled some kind of talcum powder on your punctures."

"This—this party who visited me was bound to do something for me," he muttered. "I told this party I was all right, but they went right ahead."

Justina poured cold liniment on his hide so lavishly that he groaned through his teeth. "Was this party Mrs. Hughson?" she asked.

"Now that I think back, I believe it was."

"It's strange you'd let her do anything for you. Will Mr. Hughson send his superintendent to treat you next time?"

Rian sat up. Her face was flushed. "I felt just like you do," he said. "That she might pour wolf's-bane on me. But she was talking, so I let her. I got plenty out of her, too."

"Ha!" the girl scoffed. "I expect she got more out of you than you realize, too. What did you find out?"

"Things I already knew—that they're out to kill me. And things I didn't know. I'll tell you about them some other time."

"Oh, I'm not prying," Justina said. "Suit yourself—tell me any time you feel like it. It's really

82

no business of mine, since we aren't actually partners."

Rian lay down again. "Let's get these Shackley marks covered up," he said. "The air hurts them. I meant to bring up that partnership deal. Still interested?"

"Yes."

"I've been back and forth through your books today. Do you know there's over eight hundred dollars outstanding?"

"Of course."

"Then why don't you collect it?"

"We've tried. Potter, the feed man, has stalled us for six months. The other big account, Meanley's Hardware, is nearly a year delinquent. But Father refuses to take them to court, because we owe people, too, and he's afraid it might stir them up against us."

"But you only owe a couple of hundred. Do you think Potter has the money, if he wanted to pay?"

"He owns half the real estate in this town! Of course he could pay."

"Tomorrow morning I'll collect from Potter then."

"How?"

"I'll just walk in and ask for the money," Rian said.

"Rian, you actually don't dare leave this room, and you know it!" Justina protested. "For the last two days I've seen Artie Judd on the street every time I've been out. And he's carrying a gun—that ugly tortoise-shell thing."

"I think it's real pretty. I liked carrying it myself.

And I'm not afraid of it, so it won't be keeping me in my room."

"Well—but there's still Shackley, and that filthy little offscrapings called Spence. And Hughson."

"My problems, lady, not yours. If you think I can't handle them, maybe you'd better not tie up with me."

Justina was silent while she finished her task.

"I hope you can handle them, Rian. I don't know how any one man can handle an army like Hughson's, though."

"It's not an army. Just a rabble. Have we got a deal?"

Justina rose, rinsed her hands, and walked to the door. She turned. "Yes. I'll have the papers drawn up tomorrow."

"Fine." Rian frowned as he noticed something missing from the dresser. "Where's my whiskey?"

"In my handbag. It's probably poisoned. Even if it isn't, it won't help for you to be staggering around town while they're hunting you."

Rian smiled as he lolled on the cot. "I'm beginning to think you care, Tina."

"I do—about my investments. Good night."

In the morning, Rian made a list.

At the top of the list was the name Potter, Ira. He had a haircut and a shave, used his remaining thirty cents for breakfast, and strolled down to Potter's Feed Barn. It was ten o'clock. The town was redolent of warm, sweet smells and the blackbirds set up a mighty twittering. Rian felt good. His back was stiff with scar tissue and he was somewhat groggy, but with every stride he felt stronger and more confident.

He kept an eye out for Artie Judd or any others of the Hughson crowd. Reaching the feed barn, a high, square pile of adobe with a sheet-metal roof, he entered through a large sliding door and peered around the gloomy interior. In long racks were open barrels of feed piled to the rafters with baled hay.

As he stood there, he heard the twittering of barn swallows darting in and out through the door to their nests of mud anchored to the ceiling rafters. There was a rich smell of molasses feed, and the sun shafted long blurred beams through the dusty air.

"Anybody home?" he bawled.

From a door in one wall, an old man's voice called, "Right in here!"

Rian wandered into the office. There were two sections: a countered area in the forepart, a curtained cubbyhole in the back. No one but an elderly bookkeeper was in view. With a pen in his hand, a statement before him, he looked up. He was neat and smallish, rather wistful-looking in his black suit with braid binding its edges and a high white collar sawing away at the underside of his jaws.

"Was there something?" he asked.

Rian leaned on the counter. "Boss man around?"

"No. He'll be back, oh, around noon."

"I see—my name's McCool. I'm with Empire Stage—their new partner."

With a small clatter, the pen dropped on the desk. The old man's mouth fell open. "Mister—*McCool?*" he asked.

"You know about me?"

The old man shook his head, changed his mind and nodded; then he said hastily, "Look, Mister McCool, we do business with Shackley's outfit, sell him most of his feed in fact, but I—I just work here."

Rian shrugged. "That's up to you. All I want is the six hundred dollars Potter owes us. By the way, what's your name?"

"Moore. I'm the bookkeeper."

A chair scraped in the back office. Rian gazed sternly at Moore. "Thought you said the boss wasn't here?"

Moore's pouched eyes wavered. "Why—well, you see—"

Rian got the picture: Potter was not in unless he elected to be. At that moment a very corpulent man with a large, naked-looking nose appeared in the door of the private office. He wore a black suit with a half-dozen lodge buttons on the lapel, and his red, glazed features were set in a half-frightened, half-angry cast.

"Moore," he said, "I've got to run down to the bank. Tell Mr. Potter I've gone to check on a new account."

Moore murmured something. Potter—for Rian had no doubt it was he—pushed through the counter gate and headed out.

When he had departed, Rian said, "That's him, eh?"

"Yes, sir."

Rian touched a frayed place on the edge of Moore's coat lapel. "How's the pay here? Better than it is for his creditors, I hope."

"It's tolerable, Mr. McCool." Moore's voice tried to be casual but rang with misery.

"Reason I asked is that we need a bookkeeper very bad. Pay will be ten dollars more than Potter pays you—for a starter."

"Don't Miss Justina do the bookwork for Dan?"

Rian chuckled. "Women are wonderful in the kitchen, Mr. Moore, but they can sure play hell with a set of books. She hasn't sent out any regular statements in months. I'm changing everything. First job is to start suit on delinquent accounts. Does Potter have any money?"

Moore came to the counter. His hands were trembling slightly and he linked his fingers to control them.

"Mr. McCool, he owns half the real estate in town," he said, using the same time-hallowed phrase Justina had used. "He doesn't pay because Mr. Hughson don't want him to. Hughson would transfer his feed account if he did. He's in pretty thick with George, I'm afraid. I—I believe George is a little in arrears to us, you see. For over a thousand dollars. And our best chance of collecting will come after the Reeses quit."

"But they aren't going to quit," Rian said. "I'll testify to that. Do you want that job?"

"Can—can I have a week to think about it? A man my age don't like to plunge in cold."

"You're not so old, Mr. Moore. That man-my-age talk will age a man fast, though. No, in a week I'll have somebody else on the job. I'm sorry. We've got to make hay while the sun shines. Get some money coming in fast."

Moore chewed his lip. At length he said in a whisper, "All right. I'll take it!"

Rian squeezed his hand. "Good. Now your first job is to advise me on how to go about getting that money out of Potter."

Passing his hand over his thin gray hair, Moore muttered, "If I was you, McCool, I'd take the books while he's out. Then, don't you see, he can't send out any statements to collect money people owe *him*! Why, he'd be in a devil of a spot. He'd more'n likely trot right over with the six hundred—plus delinquent penalties, of course."

Rian slapped him on the shoulder. "You're all right, Mr. Moore. What's your first name?"

"Bob."

"Well, Bob, suppose you get a cardboard box about so big and put the books in it. Then take them down to the Empire office and tell Justina you're working for us and for her to hide the books."

"I'd rather you took them yourself, Mr. Mc-Cool."

"No one'll see them, and besides I'm going to be busy."

"How so?"

"By now Potter will have told Hughson I'm up and about, and Hughson will be sending Judd out to find me. Liable to be a busy morning for me."

He laid Dan Reese's gun on the counter and checked the loads. "Not that I look for any real trouble, but they aren't above pulling another bluff. And I'm not above calling it."

Moore put the ledgers in a box and laid a newspaper over them. He collected all his little possessions—pipes, tobacco, and the like—from his drawer. With a nod to Rian, he went out.

Thirty seconds later, as Rian finished checking the gun, he was back, white as paper.

"You're right, Mr. McCool! Artie Judd and Biff Shackley are standing in front of the stage depot, looking this way!"

# Chapter Twelve

RIAN GAVE THE old man ten minutes to slip out the side door of the feed barn and make his way to the Empire office. He did not want him involved in what might happen in the street.

As he went toward the street door, he felt his heart sledging in the cage of his ribs. For an instant he was giddy; he reached out and steadied himself against a barrel while his head cleared. He had been in bed too long, was still too drawn out like a wire, for sudden excitement.

Yet it was not fear, but a sort of elation, that he experienced. As yet he could not strike directly at Hughson, but he was coming closer all the time.

He stepped into the street. The feed barn was at the north end of the business district, and on the east side of the street. The stage office was near the middle of the town, perhaps a hundred yards south, on the opposite side of the street. There was very little traffic—a cowboy jogging in from a cross street, a heavy freight truck rumbling into an alley, a dozen people on the walks.

He saw a large, slope-shouldered man in a shirt striped like a barber's apron on the east side of the street, opposite Hughson's depot. He recognized his black trousers and yellow boots; he thought he discerned even the lavender sleeve-garters of Hughson's gunman, Artie Judd. Judd was standing in the sunlight, staring toward the feed barn.

Sitting in one of the alcoved windows of the depot was Biff Shackley. The big super saw McCool and came to his feet. Like Judd, he wore a gun.

Rian walked down the sidewalk toward Judd. There were cement curbs, but the walk itself was dirt, deeply scalloped by the feet of pedestrians. When he had gone about a hundred feet, he stepped into the street and started on a diagonal toward Shackley. Judd came to the edge of the curb, as Shackley, too, came forward. They had him in a beautiful crossfire.

He wondered whether Judd had discovered that he had no effective firing pin in his weapon.

*God help me if he's fixed it!* he thought.

It was in his mind to walk toward Shackley, passing him without stepping into the walk—unless Shackley went for his gun. If he did, he would deal with him.

When he was just short of Shackley, with Judd in the tail of his eye, the superintendent suddenly bawled, "Last chance, McCool! Turn back and take off or you're done."

"Turn my back on the likes of you?" said Rian.

He kept walking.

Judd called, "Count of three, horsebreaker! One—"

At the count of three, Rian saw Shackley's hand move. His heart leaped painfully; he drew his ancient, borrowed Colt. From Judd's position he heard a *click*, then a curse. He saw the sun glint on Shackley's revolver; then the gun in his own hand uttered a terrible roar and almost jumped from his fingers. A dense fog of powder smoke sprang up between them. The roar of the gun was an unmanning thing. Through the heavy, rolling echoes he heard Judd's gun click twice more; then there was an angry shout from the gunman.

He heard nothing from Shackley. But as the smoke drifted aside he saw him sitting heavily on the walk, his back against the wall of the station. The gun lay a few feet from his hand.

Rian turned toward Judd. The gunman screamed, "You dirty rat!" and backed off.

Keeping the Colt trained on him, Rian walked forward, Judd collided with the wall. Once more he raised the gun and pointed it at Rian.

Rian laughed.

Artie Judd turned abruptly and ran a few yards to an alley, ducked into it and was out of sight.

Another man was on the walk now, tall, slender, grim. He carried a shotgun, and there was a shield on his coat.

"This is loaded with nuts and bolts, McCool," he

said. "Don't make me turn the town's stomach. Put your gun away."

Rian sighed and lowered the Colt. "Yes, sir," he said.

"I told you before," Marshal Fowley said, "that I wouldn't stand for any nonsense from you." They were in the marshal's office, with five or six men grouped about the room, peering at Rian, among them the newspaper editor, the marshal's deputy, and the coroner.

"This nonsense wasn't my idea," Rian said. "They were waiting for me. Ask Bob Moore."

"I'll question Moore," Fowley said sternly. "Also Judd, when I find him."

Outside, there was a brisk sound of a woman's footsteps, and Justina came into the doorway. The men removed their hats and murmured grave greetings as she entered the room. Fowley rose from his desk.

"Miss Justina, can you come back later? I'm conducting an investigation."

Pushing at a loose strand of hair—she looked as though she had just been putting her hair up when the firing started—she gave him a weak smile. "I heard that my partner was involved in a shooting—"

Fowley turned his head on the side. "Your partner?"

"Mr. McCool."

The marshal looked at Rian, and sighed. "You move fast, McCool."

"In this town," Rian said, "you've got to move fast to keep alive. Are you going to lock me up?"

"No. Since it *appears* that you were the victim instead of the criminal. But there'll be a coroner's inquest, of course, and you'll either be bound over or freed, depending on the jury's findings."

Rian heard Justina let out a sigh. There was high color in her face, and as he studied her he saw her clench her hands with nervousness. Somehow he had the feeling that her visit to the marshal's office was not entirely tied to the shooting.

"Can he leave then?" the girl asked quickly.

Fowley nodded.

"With or without gun?" Rian asked. "It doesn't belong to me, actually. Besides, I'd feel kind of naked without it, with people sniping at me all the time."

Fowley picked the revolver up, sniffed the barrel, scowled, and finally shrugged. "Keep the damned—your pardon, Miss Justina—keep the thing in your holster," he warned. He offered it, butt first.

Hurrying along the walk beside Rian, Justina glanced back as if to make sure they were not being followed. Then she clutched his arm and looked up at him.

"Rian, we're finished!"

"We were finished before we ever teamed up," Rian said. "This outfit is plumb snakebit. But what's new?"

"Our Frontera office was robbed last night."

He stopped and smiled at her. "What'd we lose—couple of cans of saddle soap and a beat-up horse?"

"Three thousand dollars in gold!"

Rian blinked. "What've you been doing—hiding assets from me?"

"It wasn't our money. It belonged to a mercury mining company. The money was supposed to come here on the stage tomorrow, under special guard. Mr. Brogan, our supervisor, rode down to tell us."

"Where is he?"

"He's at home, with Father."

"Let's talk to him."

Brogan was a tall old man with a skull-like head and face. His shoulders were unnaturally broad, like the framework on which a much larger man was to be constructed. Loops of brownish skin had collected under his eyes. He was sitting on the horsehair sofa with his hat in his hands, looking solemn and defeated.

Rian knew immediately that he would have to fire the man as soon as he could replace him. You could not build a fire with wet wood.

"Well, sir, it was all over so fast I can't hardly tell you how many there was of them," Brogan said. "There was this knock. I'd just looked up. 'Who's that?' I says. 'This is Shorty, from the stable,' somebody says. Well, sir, there is a Shorty at Meyers' stable, so—"

He told how three men had come in, tied him up, and carried off the cashbox.

"Why wasn't it locked in the safe?" asked Rian.

"I was just putting it away," Brogan explained. "The mine manager brought it down at six o'clock. This was about six-thirty."

"Anybody try to follow them?"

"I told the county sheriff, and he organized a little posse. But they couldn't turn nothing up."

Justina sniffed. "That fat old sheriff! I'll wager he never wasted much time looking."

"About an hour, miss," said Brogan.

"The first place to look would be along the river," Justina said. "That's the way everything stolen slides, like the county was sloped that way. They hide everything from stolen mercury flasks to bank loot in the caves, and take it across the river after they've made arrangements in Mexico. What shall we do, Mr. McCool? We'll have to make that loss good."

"Don't you have insurance?"

"No. We're too small to qualify."

Rian told Brogan, "You might as well head back, Mr. Brogan. We'll put it in the hands of a U. S. marshal if we can ever get one down here."

"If there's anything I can do—" said Brogan.

*The only thing you can do is eat and sleep, like a spavined horse*, thought Rian. He said, "No, thanks. We'll mule along somehow."

After the man left, he said, "Draw me a little map of that cave section. I'll ride up the river right now and poke around."

While he assembled a few things—a couple of blankets in case he got caught out at night, some food in a paper sack—she started on a map. Then, with an exclamation, she threw it in the fireplace.

"I can't tell you where to go. I'll have to show you. It would take you three days to find the spot by yourself. There are more blind alleys than you could imagine."

Rian shook his head, the blanket roll of provisions over his shoulder. "I'm not taking any helpless females along," he muttered. "Dan, you got a rifle?"

Dan Reese lifted a repeating rifle from pegs over the fireplace and dug a box of shells from a drawer. "She ain't so helpless," he said. "Tina grew up in them caves. I was ranching over there till she was thirteen. Only worry you'd have is keeping up with her."

Rian scowled. Justina hurried into her bedroom; he could hear her pulling things from the closet. Rian lowered his voice. "What if we have to spend the night out there?"

"Let me worry about that," Justina called from the bedroom. "I may be frail, but I can fight like a tiger."

"I'll saddle your horses," said Dan.

Fifteen minutes later, Justina emerged from the house dressed in a girl's Levis, a shirt of her father's under a denim jacket, and high-heeled boots. She carried a small buggy rifle in addition to a blanket roll. There was a fragrance of rose water about her as Rian held her stirrup for her.

"I hope you brought along plenty of perfume," he said. "You can't hardly find a store over that way, I hear."

Stiff-necked, he rode from the yard to the side street Justina followed, riding loose and easy in the saddle, her hair pinned up in a tight coronet, and a kerchief drawn over her head. It was about twelve-thirty. McCool figured they could make the ten-mile ride in about three hours.

# Chapter Thirteen

"YOU THICK-HEADED pistol jockey!" Hughson said bitterly. He sat on the deep window-sill of his office, scowling at Artie Judd, who sat at Hughson's desk. Judd looked up, his face dark with frustration and a rage turned inward. Judd was holding his pistol in his two hands.

"But look at this thing, George! How could I have—?"

Hughson made a quick, savage gesture. "I've looked at it! And I've looked at you till I'm sick of looking at both of you. You're drawing more pay than anybody in this outfit, and yet all I've asked of you was to make a noise like a gun when I pulled the trigger. Hell!" he snorted. "As long as the competition was an old man and a girl, you looked great.

But as soon as a jailbird with a fourth-grade education came along, you started firing low, high, and sideways."

Judd's baffled anger was still focused on the gun. "If you'd wanted him killed the day he got out of jail, why didn't you say so?"

"I didn't want him killed! Not then—not until you'd fouled the machinery so that nothing but killing would stop him. And *then*, damn it, you bungled again!"

Shackley was dead. Potter was on the run and would probably be putting six hundred dollars operating cash into the Reeses' hands tomorrow. Yet things were stirring nicely down the river in Frontera, and if he acted the part of a man in trouble, it was largely to stimulate Judd to more effective action.

Judd snapped the hammer of the Colt twice, and shook his head.

"Why don't you pack your gear and head out?" Hughson suggested.

Judd frowned. "Don't you want me to check with Spence and see how things went?"

"I know how they went. The stage office in Frontera was robbed last night. What else do I need to know?"

"Whether Spence and the others got away clean. Makin' it out of town ain't getting away, necessarily."

Hughson shrugged and walked to the desk. Quickly, the gunman vacated the chair. Hughson pulled a drawer open and took a handful of cigars from a box, which he tucked into the breast pocket of his coat.

"What're you going to do?" asked Judd.

"Go down to Frontera and see what's happening."

"Nothin'll happen there," Judd told him. "They done made it to the river, at least."

Hughson snapped an impatient look at him.

"The point is, somebody may try to make a federal case out of it. They do handle mail in that office, you know. According to what Morton told me, he'll be in Frontera this week, heading back to El Paso. If he's around town, I want to talk to him. He's the one who'll decide who handles the matter: the local law, or the U. S. marshal's office in El Paso."

Hughson reached into a closet and took out a Colt hanging from a nail in a plain black holster. His brow wrinkled. Judd watched him buckle it on.

"I'll ride up with you," he said.

"Suit yourself."

Judd spoke eagerly. "Tell you what: I'll ride as far as Carrizo Creek and cut over to the river, see what news I can pick up. Okay?"

Without meeting his eager look, yet acknowledging by a softening of his tone that Judd was being given a final chance, Hughson growled:

"Suit yourself. If you see Spence, tell him to sit tight for a day or two, and then head back. But before you go anywhere, you'd better hike over to Dominguez' shop and get a new firing pin put in that gun hammer."

The gunman left. Hughson sat down and made notes of things he wanted to accomplish in Frontera. He heard a slight sound and glanced up.

Abby stood in the doorway. She wore a black

gown which nipped her waist, a double strand of pearls at her throat. The black enhanced the fairness of her skin, made her look pallid and somehow vulnerable, and Hughson felt a stab of the old intense desire he had had for her early in their marriage. It came to him suddenly to enjoy her before leaving town. He dropped his pencil and stood up.

Abby entered the room. Hughson, smiling faintly, moved to close the door. She watched him as he came toward her. He held her by the elbows and looked into her face.

"Black becomes you, Abby," he said. "Why don't you wear it more often?"

"Perhaps I shall. Poor Mr. Shackley," Abby sighed.

He was immediately annoyed. But he pulled her against him quickly and kissed her. She turned her face away with that infuriating way women had of sharpening a man's passion while they ignored it.

"For Heaven's sake!" she gasped. "Is this how we're going to meet our business problems?"

"It's one way," he said, smiling.

"A better way," his wife said, "might be to sell out and move somewhere else. I'm fed up, George. I hate this town and the people, and I hate losing money!"

His hands slipped down to her waist and he held her when she tried to move away.

"Move where? By the time we got through paying bills, we'd be washed out. Rule One of this business is that you must have a mail contract to make money. A thousand dollars a mile—and it's eighteen miles to Frontera. You'll have to take this on faith, but in a month we'll have the field to ourselves, contract and all."

His hand moved to the small of her back, while his lips sought the soft perfumed skin of her neck. After a moment Abby pushed him away and stepped back.

"Men!" she said. "While you're talking business, you're scheming how to get a girl's clothes off her."

There was a hidden meaning in her words; he knew her too well to let the remark pass. "Who else has been talking business to you lately?" he asked.

She gazed at him. "Rian McCool," she said. "He came to me with the craziest plan. He said that if you died, I'd own all the property. That's true, of course. But you aren't going to die—are you?"

Hughson said huskily, "You—you—you're making this up! You haven't even seen him."

Her lips turned up in a teasing smile. "I took him some whiskey while he was sick—something to while away the time. Maybe it was just the whiskey talking; he got drunk before I knew what was happening. Gracious, he's more man half dead than most men are with all their faculties! *Are* you going to die, George?" she asked earnestly.

Hughson reached inside his coat and drew the gun he carried on his left hip. He walked to Abby, staring into her face, and placed the muzzle of the gun against her breast.

"I feel pretty healthy, Abby," he said. "How about you?"

"Never better, George. I wrote a letter telling how well I felt, mentioning the possibility of an accident.

I left it with an attorney."

He knew he was hurting her; he could see it in the pinch-lines about her eyes.

"So what you thought," he scoffed, "was that you could prod me into a showdown with McCool, eh? And then you could turn the poor slob down, if he had the luck to kill me. Or if I killed him, they'd hang me for it, eh? Abby, don't take cards in a man's game. A woman gets her bluff called every time."

He stepped back, holstered the gun, and went behind his desk. He locked it, tossed the key and caught it, and walked out.

# Chapter Fourteen

THE SMELL IN the air was of damp earth and rotting vegetation. Rian and the girl had left the county road an hour earlier, ridden south to the river road, and were following its slow kinks southeast through jungles of mesquite and thickets of the heavy yellow cane, locally called *higar*.

Justina explained that it was very good feed. On her suggestion, her father had had some Mexicans cut and truss tons of it and haul it to town. Potter had bought it for six hundred dollars and never paid for it. But she still thought it was good business.

"Now that we're going to be paid for it," she said happily.

The road consisted of two wandering tracks lurching over roots and rocks, boggy here and there with mossy seeps of river water. A stone's throw to their right lay the wide, shallow Rio Grande, islanded with sand bars. The land was generally flat, but ahead Rian could see low cliffs split by the river. They had not discussed the implications of the robbery. But both of them knew that Empire Stage Lines would die in twenty-four hours if they had to make good on a three-thousand-dollar loss. Every creditor in town would be serving them with papers, trying to get his money before they folded.

Justina halted her horse, gazing at a giant mesquite as big as an Eastern oak. "Rian, I used to climb that tree and pretend I was an Army scout," she sighed. "You can see miles down the river, and across into Mexico. Sometimes I'd see smuggler trains coming or going. Once some mercury smugglers passed right under the tree!"

"Fine place for a girl to be," commented Rian.

"Oh, they're harmless enough—just poor peasants trying to make a living. If they'd seen me, they'd have tipped their hats and said, *'Que tal, señorita?'* and ridden on."

"I've got a feeling these men won't be so polite."

"So have I. That's why I'm going to climb the tree and see what I can see." She raised her arm to point south. "The main trail into Chihuahua crossed the river right there. But there are a dozen trails to the crossing on this side. Some of them start in Santa Cruz canyon—the cliffs you see. There are a thousand little side canyons leading into the main one."

Rian dismounted. "Boys first," he said. "I've got a good nose for anybody that's lashed up with

Hughson. They give off a certain smell."

Justina shrugged and dismounted while he pulled off boots and socks to climb the big tree. He studied it a moment. It was a perfect climbing tree, with frequent stout limbs and not too much foliage. The leaves were small, like those of a mountain ash. He climbed; it was almost like ascending stairs. High in the tree he found a fork where he wedged himself.

Eastward, toward Frontera, the land rolled away, as brown and wrinkled as an old hide. "I can see smoke about ten miles east," he said.

Justina was lying on her back to look up at him. "That's the smelter at the mercury mines. What do you see in Mexico?"

He looked for dust, the sparkle of harness fastenings, the gleam of leather. In the dun vastness sweeping out to some distant blue mountains, islanded with small, flattopped mesas, he saw nothing.

He called his findings down to her.

"Good," she said. "Maybe they aren't going to move the money at all. They might just hide it here till the fuss blows over."

"Hey!" Rian called softly, peering toward the reddish cliffs where the river entered Santa Cruz Canyon. "There's some smoke over in the canyon."

Justina scrambled up. "How far down?"

"Can't say. It looks like it's from the main canyon."

"I'm coming up," the girl called.

Soon she was standing beside him, scrutinizing the river canyon. "It's in Oso Negro Canyon," she said. "That comes into the main canyon about half a mile below the cliffs. It might be cowboys, but I doubt it."

"Why?"

"Too early for a supper fire, and there's no branding going on now. It's more than likely someone who sits around making coffee and eating while he waits for a message."

"I'll have a look." Rian started back down the tree.

Justina came right behind him. "They'd eat you alive, Rian. You don't know the trails. We'll go together."

Artie Judd had left the county road an hour earlier and ridden into the thickets running out to the river. It was hot in the brush, and a cloud of gnats traveled with him, getting into his ears and the corners of his eyes. "Damn insects!" he muttered, swatting at the gnats in his ears.

He came from the brush onto a silty road paralleling the river, stopped and scowled in thought. Judd had been this way only once. Spence had brought him there and showed him some caves where, if he ever needed to hide out for a while, there was always a supply of canned food, matches, and hooks and line for taking channel cat.

A thought crossed his mind, and he grinned to himself.

Why not knock over Spence, if he was alone, and take off with the money? Nobody would ever be in a position to report the crime to the authorities; nor could they ever hang it on him.

But he felt obscurely obligated to George Hughson. He had drawn a good salary for months for doing nothing but crowd a wagon off the grade, now and then, or muscle a driver around until he quit the Reese line and left town. Now he'd been called on to earn his keep. But he'd bungled it twice—because of McCool. As much as obligation, therefore, he felt a prodding urge to square with McCool before he left.

Not much of a tracker, Judd had ridden a hundred yards before he discovered that he was following another rider. He slipped to the ground and looked at the hoofprints.

Two horses, by God! The sign was sharp-edged and fresh. Judd swung back into the saddle. Rubbing his jaw, he gazed down the river. Nothing in sight, and the earth was too damp to show dust.

He pulled the rifle from the scabbard under his knee and rode ahead.

The river had scoured away at the red walls of Santa Cruz Canyon until it achieved a winding cleft little more than a hundred feet wide. The broad and shallow reach of muddy water became a narrow stream flecked with foam as it traveled with a low rumble of power. There was a trail littered with driftwood on the American side of the stream. A wind smelling of dampness blew against their faces as Rian and the girl rode down the canyon.

Rian shot apprehensive glances about them. He did not like the sensation of being boxed in. He feared an exposed back-trail and the unknown trail ahead. The cliffs were sheer and red, with a few tufts of Spanish bayonet clinging to them.

Several times he stopped and looked for hoofprints. But he saw none until they reached the confluence of Oso Negro Canyon. Here he saw several sets of prints leading from the side canyon to the rocks at the river's edge.

"Reckon they crossed here?" he asked.

Justina shook her head, raising her voice to be heard over the eerie fluting of wind and the rumble of water.

"It's ten feet deep and going forty miles an hour," she told him. "They just came down to water their horses and go back. It might have been cowboys."

"Any caves in the canyon? he asked.

"It's full of them."

He scrutinized the smaller canyon with its craggy cliffs and heavy thickets, then glanced back the way they had come.

"Stay here while I go ahead," he said. "If anybody comes along, fire a shot to stop them. Then ride up the side canyon and we'll take off."

She shook her head. "I'm the general here, Rian. You stay. I know every cave between here and Frontera. Give me ten minutes. If nobody comes, ride up and meet me. I'll wait for you. Then I'll ride ahead another ten minutes."

He shrugged and let her go.

Dismounting, he led his horse fifty yards up Oso Negro Canyon and tied it. He went back and pried himself into a wedge between two boulders, from which he could watch the back trail.

Less than a hundred yards west, the canyon made one of its sharp kinks and the trail disappeared

behind rubble and willows. His skin crawled; the
whole layout was perfect for disaster. Anyone
following them would see him almost as soon as he
was seen. The river sounds would bury the echoes of
gunfire a hundred yards away. If anything did
happen, and their escape was blocked in this
direction, it might easily be blocked in Oso Negro
Canyon as well.

He glanced at his watch. Five minutes. Justina
had no timepiece; if her time sense was not better
than most women's, she might ride a half-hour
before she stopped to wait for him.

He looked over his borrowed rifle. It was an old
trap-door Springfield with specks of rust on it. He
wondered whether the loads were as ancient as the
gun. To check on the caps, he opened the breech of
the gun. His fingertip rubbed the cap of the shell in
the chamber; smooth and clean. Then, just as he
started to throw the bolt home, he heard a shod hoof
strike a stone.

Startled, he ducked down into the cleft. Presently
he raised himself a few inches and scrutinized the
trail. He saw nothing, and again shoved at the rifle
bolt. It would not slide. He swore, opened the
breech again, and once more pushed at the bolt.
Once more it jammed.

As the hoof sounds grew suddenly louder, he
looked up to see Artie Judd riding around the turn.
The burly gunman had his hat pushed back; he
carried a rifle like a man expecting to need it at any
moment.

Rian groaned, ducked down and worked with
the rifle again. Failing to break the jam, he dropped

it and drew his Colt. Judd was within a hundred feet. Suddenly, on some instinct, he reined in and raised his rifle. His gaze came to rest on Rian.

Rian threw off a quick shot, the canyon exploded into tumbling echoes and Judd's horse began to pitch. The gunman fired as he fought the horse. Rian backed out of the cleft and ran hunched over for his horse. A bullet slashed the air above him. He whirled, fired at the gunman. Judd reined into cover as Rian ran again.

He untied the horse, hit the saddle, and rode up the side canyon.

# Chapter Fifteen

A HALF MILE up the canyon, a horseman reined quickly into the trail before him. He raised his old revolver, but it was Justina.

"Rian! What is it?" she asked.

"Judd's behind me! If he's here, there must be others. How do we get out of this canyon?"

He stared up at the craggy cliffs, stained red and green with minerals. Broken by erosion, they were littered with boulders and tough desert shrubs.

Justina frowned. "We could ride straight on up the canyon, but I just saw the smoke. It's a few hundred yards ahead. Wait—"

She rode a few yards ahead and turned her horse into the brush on the left side of the canyon. Beyond her, Rian perceived a curl of blue-gray smoke twisting into the air. At the top of the cliffs, the wind bent it southeast.

"There's a cow trail here," Justina called. "Come on."

The trail ran along the rubbled base of the north cliff, then began climbing gradually. He could see several faint trails scraped into the sloping canyon wall by the hoofs of cattle and deer.

They had climbed fifty feet from the canyon floor when the first shot crashed into the baked-earth slope behind them. The horses bucked. Up through the brush and rocks came the smashing report of a rifle shot. Rian cursed the inoperative rifle on his saddle as he pulled the Colt. Down on the narrow canyon floor he could see a smear of black powder, and he fired at it.

Justina spurred her horse, but the frightened animal merely set its legs and quivered. Another slug smashed through a creosote bush at Rian's side. This shot came from farther up the canyon. Looking down, he could see the wood smoke where someone was camped; the shot had come from nearby. He gazed up and saw that before they ever reached the top they would be exposed on the hillside like flies on a wall.

He jumped down and led his horse ahead. "Get down!" he told the girl. "We've got to take cover."

White as paper, she gazed at him. Rian gave her a shake. "Come on! We've got to get out of here."

Justina turned her head. "There's a cave up here," she whispered. "I—I think it's on this trail."

He led his horse past hers and ran up the trail. Glancing back, he saw her following him. Another shot ripped the brush and wailed off a rock by the trial.

He came to a cave, and was staring bleakly into it as Justina hurried up beside him. "You must have been pretty young when you called this a cave," he said.

The floor, covered with rocks, ran into the hill about twenty feet to meet the back wall. This wall rose vertically for a few feet, then sloped forward to become the ceiling. Thus there was no shelter from above, but they could lead the horses back to safety and lie behind the rocks at the front.

Without a word he took the girl's reins from her and led both horses into the shelter. Down below he heard a man shout; from another point someone answered. Spence and Judd were identifying themselves to one another.

He took the little buggy rifle from Justina's saddle and placed her behind a rock. Another shot glanced off the stones below the mouth of the cave. Through the cascade of echoes, he fired three fast shots at the smoke and crouched to reload. While he punched out the smoking shells, he told Justina:

"My rifle's jammed. See if you can clear it. Damn thing's rusted solid."

She worked at the bolt, then pulled a hairpin from the crown of her braids and began futilely picking at the follower mechanism.

"Rian," she whispered, "how are we going to get out of here?"

Rian took her chin between his thumb and forefinger. He kissed her solidly, and let her pull back, astonished.

"Well, we could take a horsecar," he said, "but I thought we'd wait till night and make a run for it. And hope one of those knotheads don't have sense enough to go for help."

Touching her mouth, she asked, "Why did you do that?"

"What if I get my head blown off in the next five minutes? It'd be awful to die *without* doing it. I've been thinking about it for quite some time."

"I think you're crazy," she said.

"Probably. Be thinking of where this trail goes, too. I want a little map of it—scratch it in the dirt, if you can find any."

The shots came sporadically—two or three, then silence. Rocked with thunderous echoes, the cliff seemed to tremble. Suddenly Justina exclaimed with pleasure.

"It works! Look—there was a twig jammed into it."

Rian took the gun, worked the trap-door breech several times, and nodded approvingly. He spilled out half the box of old corroded shells beside him and loaded the gun.

Laying the rifle barrel across a rock, he tried to see what was going on down in the canyon. Shadows obscured the lower trail. When a gun was fired, he saw the flash, and ducked. A moment later the slug struck the sloping roof of the cave and ricocheted around. Justina gasped and pressed against him.

The shot had come from up-canyon, where the wolfish little gunman named Spence was holed up. Rian remembered him that night when Shackley whipped him—a coyote of a man with cold yellow eyes. He held his breath to steady the gun, looking for a flash of movement. Again he saw the yellow stab of flame and he fired quickly and ducked. With an earsplitting concussion, the other man's shot struck the rock before him and caromed off the ceiling of the cave.

"Let's have that map," Rian muttered. "We may have to get out of here before dark."

The girl moved back and smoothed the earth with her hand. Taking a sharp pebble from the floor, she sketched the canyon. Rian glanced at the lines in the earth. Dusk was blurring details in the cave.

"This is where we are," she said. "Another little gully comes in here—it must be a couple of hundred yards. The gully tops out in the hills. The road's over here."

Rian nodded, squirmed around and got comfortable again. In the brush tangle below, someone was moving toward the trail to the caves. He took a rough aim, and fired two shots. The horses snorted and stamped.

The shots came more frequently now; the men had worked in closer to the cave. Uneasily, Rian realized that the cave was now in a cross fire. They would be under fire till dark; sooner or later, one of the snipers would get lucky.

"We've got to take off," he said suddenly. "Bring the horses and check the cinches."

Justina led the horses forward while he reloaded. When she had mounted, he fired the whole magazine of his rifle. The canyon rocked with echoes. No shots came back; it was apparent that the gunmen were riding out the volley under cover. He mounted quickly. From the cave mouth he fired two revolver shots before riding on up the cattle trail.

Once the hoof sounds echoed through the canyon, the gunfire below broke out with a reverberating clamor. Rian spurred his horse. Stumbling over the rocks, it bucked and lunged along the narrow cattle trail.

There was a wicked smack behind him.

Justina's horse uttered a loud grunt and went down. Rian saw the girl land in the tangle of creosote brush and begin to struggle. Swearing under his breath, he rode his horse back and reached an arm down to her, kicking free of his stirrup. She toed into the stirrup and swung up behind him. He lashed the horse with the reins.

After a few moments the girl gasped, "The side canyon's just ahead."

It was hardly more than a scar on the side of the main canyon. He could see where the run-off of summer rains had raked a notch in the earth. As he turned the horse, the guns opened up below them. In a few moments the arroyo deepened. The shots were passing high over their heads now.

Twenty minutes later they topped out among some broken hills. They stopped and dismounted to rest the horse. Rian reloaded, while Justina sat on a boulder with her face buried in her hands.

"You know," he said, "if I'd known how you ran stage lines down here, I might have gone into another line of work."

# Chapter Sixteen

"THIS IS MR. SHARP, manager of Texas Mining Industries," Wiley Brogan said uneasily. Brogan, Justina's manager in Frontera, extended a hand of introduction toward a small, rawhide-tough little man with a brown face and black flint-chips of eyes.

It was midmorning, and they were gathered in the stage office—Rian, Justina, Brogan, and Sharp. Rian and the girl had reached town about midnight and roused Brogan, who procured rooms for them.

Justina, who knew the mining man, smiled at him as Rian offered his hand. Sharp peered into Rian's face, nodded brusquely, and took a cigar from his pocket. It was his company whose three thousand dollars had been stolen, and he had asked a meeting to discuss the matter.

"What about the money?" he asked shortly.

"We're making every effort to track it down," Justina said. "We have some leads—"

"You've got leads, and I had some money," Sharp interrupted. "What I want to know is, why the devil you people don't carry insurance to protect you against such losses."

Justina explained about insurance requirements. Sharp lighted his cigar and spun the match at a cuspidor.

"In other words," he said, "we're out our three thousand?"

"No, sir," Rian said. "Not at all. If we don't recover it, we'll make restitution."

"When?"

"Just as soon as possible."

"That's not soon enough. The money was going to El Paso to pay for a submerged pump we need in one of our mines. We need the pump now—not at your convenience."

"I understand." Rian found himself employing phrases and mannerisms he had heard successful men use.

With a serious expression, he went behind Brogan's desk and marshaled a scratch pad and a pencil. Jotting down $600, he said soberly. "We've just hired a new accountant who's going to get some things straightened out for us. Among other things, there's the matter of a thousand dollars in delinquent accounts. We took in six hundred dollars on an overdue account yesterday."

He waited, then glanced up at the mining man.

Sharp's eyes did not move from his face.

*All right so far*, Rian thought.

"We've had our problems, but we're taking steps to correct them. I'm a new partner, and I've got a background of staging."

He looked Sharp in the eye as he made the lie. In one week he had acquired more background than most men gathered in a lifetime. "We intend to stay in business despite the efforts of our competitors to drive us out."

Sharp grunted. "The Reeses have had their troubles," he agreed. "That's why I've gone along with some of their nonsense. But I can't absorb a loss like this one and keep my own job."

Rian nodded. Beneath the *$600*, he wrote: *One week from today*, and handed the slip of paper to the mining man.

"Suppose we pay you six hundred now, then two hundred a month until we've eaten up the loss? Or if we recover the money, we'll make full restitution."

In the street, a stage horn sang clean and clear. Then there was a sound of hoofs. Brogan glanced at the big Seth Thomas clock on the wall, and rubbed his jaw.

"Excuse me," he said. "Don't mean to interrupt. A man I've been waiting for is supposed to be on that stage. I want to catch him before he disappears or takes off for Kingbolt and parts west. He's a postal inspector."

"Mr. Morton?" asked Justina, in surprise.

"Why, yes," Brogan said. "According to his schedule, he'll be through on the westbound—Mr. Hughson's line, unfortunately—and I hope to get some action on this robbery. Though it wasn't a post-office loss, of course, so I can't really press him—"

Rian winced. The soft-handed approach again! *If we can't find a qualified agent to replace him*, he thought, *I'll just hire the first man I meet on the street tomorrow morning.*

"We handle mail, don't we?" Rian said sharply. "Isn't this a post-office as well as a stage line? All right, it was broken into. Mr. Sharp, what do you say to those terms?"

He moved toward the door. The stage rushed by, making for the Hughson station down the street.

Sharp's baked features wrinkled in thought. He nodded.

"It's a deal. But the first time you miss a payment I'll land on you like a cougar."


Rian hurried down the street beside Brogan, who chattered on and made little sense. Other townsmen were walking toward the depot. Frontera was a low-lying community in the broad river valley, a dun-colored town of Texas earth, and buildings made from that earth in the shape of mud bricks. It had a greater vitality than most such out-of-the-way towns had, however. Because of the mines and the trade with Mexico, there was money to be made in trading with Frontera. But not while you were fighting a war of survival.

An extremely stout man with yellowish, jaded eyes waited beside the coach as the passengers stepped from it. He was wearing a star—the "fat old sheriff" Justina had mentioned. In the doorway, a large man in a tan suit with brown velvet lapels was flipping a gold coin. He saw Rian and gave a nod and a slight smile.

Rian scowled. Hughson! When the devil had he come up? Now this was awkward. They might be able to get somewhere with Morton, but with Hughson around it would be almost impossible.

And there was Morton up on the deck, small and birdlike in his black suit, as he dusted the crown of his high derby on his sleeve. When he saw Rian, his face tried to settle on an expression of alarm or pleasure. Next he discovered George Hughson, and slowly donned his hat; now his expression was definitely one of alarm. He saw the sheriff, and pulled his shoulders in defensively.

As the postal inspector climbed down, Brogan stepped forward. "Mr. Morton, I hate to bother you but—"

The stout sheriff shouldered him aside. Brogan moved to safety, gazing at the lawman reproachfully.

"Like to talk to you, Morton," he said sternly.

Morton's features flushed. Rian could see his lips trembling. "What's the trouble, Sheriff?"

"We'll discuss it at my office."

Rian stepped up and offered his hand. "Nice to see you again, Mr. Morton," he said.

The sheriff frowned at him. "Who are you?"

"McCool. Empire Stage. I'll go along. I've got some business with Mr. Morton.

The sheriff's office, on a corner, had more flies than a stable, but it lacked the wholesome atmosphere. A water-stained cheesecloth ceiling sagged from rusty nails; the floor was of limed earth which badly needed watering down. A few dodgers were tacked to the adobe walls, where scabs of old plaster clung like mud to a hog's back.

Sheriff Murdo sat at his desk and fired up a cigar. He dropped the match on the floor and spat in a white china cuspidor.

"Now, then," he said to Rian, still wheezing from the walk. "What's your problem?"

Rian started to tell him about the robbery, but Murdo waved a fat hand and said, "I made an investigation."

"That's just it; you shouldn't have. This is a post-office case."

"Why?" George Hughson demanded. He had come along and now stood near the sheriff as if to support him.

"Because it was a post-office that they broke into."

"They didn't touch any mail. Only a private express shipment."

"Breaking into a post-office is still a federal offense." Rian looked at Sylvester Morton. "Am I right?"

There was an awkward silence. The inspector, sitting on a bench, frowned at his dusty boots. Hughson prodded him.

"Tell him, Sylvester. I'm all for tracking culprits down, but I buck against bringing in federal officers."

Morton looked up. His eyes were sad and tried. "Breaking a window in a post-office is a federal offense. This was a felony, and I'll have to call for U. S. marshals to handle it."

"Good," Rian said. "How soon can you do it?"

"I'm on my way to El Paso now. I'll make the request in person when I get there."

Hughson asked quietly, "You'll be riding the Empire stage as far as Kingbolt?"

Morton nodded. Hughson smiled. "I'll probably ride along."

Rian said, "I hope so. Our chances of getting through will be a lot better. By the way," he said, "I wanted to thank you for the bottle you sent."

Hughson squinted. "What bottle?" Then he caught the reference and turned away. "Forget it."

"No, it was a nice gesture. I was a pretty sick boy when Abby brought it. But after a couple of drinks I felt like a tiger!"

"Well, fine," Hughson said. "Sheriff—" he began. But Rian kept on, smiling persistently.

"That wife of yours! She's got a little tiger blood, too, George. I really envy you."

Everyone was looking at him now, seemingly embarrassed.

Hughson turned angrily. "There's a private matter the sheriff and I want to discuss with Morton. Will you excuse us?"

Brogan scurried out ahead of him. Rian sighed. "I really do envy you, George," he repeated. "Must keep a man stepping to keep a girl like that satisfied, though. Did I sleep the next day? I want to tell you I did!"

Hughson clenched his fists. For an instant Rian thought he was going to accept the challenge. Then he saw Hughson's glance flick to the gun on his hip, as though remembering Shackley.

Hughson wet his lips. "Get out of here," he said.

Sheriff Murdo jerked a thumb toward the door. "Take off, McCool," he ordered. "You're talking yourself into trouble."

After Rian had departed, Hughson sat on the bench beside Morton. From his billfold, he drew a check.

"I tired to cash this the other day, Morton," he murmured. "It came back marked 'insufficient funds.'"

Morton sat up straight. "You promised to hold it for two weeks!"

"Did I say that? All I know is, you'll have to pay up or go to jail."

"I can't! I'm waiting for my pay check."

"That's tough. Because I need the cash. If you haven't got it, I'll go to the district attorney."

"That's a fact," Sheriff Murdo agreed. "You'd probably lose your job, Morton."

Morton leaned back against the rough wall. "So you think you'll get a new inspector down here, eh? And he'll find out how bad things are with the Reeses and cancel them out. Is that the plan? Well, it won't work, my friends! That's where you're making your mistake."

Hughson glanced at the sheriff. "Matt, it seems to me they're making a hell of a racket down there in the cantina. Why don't you go put the gad to the animals?"

Murdo blinked. Then the idea registered and he

stood up and sauntered out. Alone with Morton, Hughson spoke frankly.

"I don't want to make trouble for you, Sylvester. But I've shown you a lot of favors, and I think it's time you reciprocated. As a matter of fact, I didn't try to cash that check. But I will—unless you and I reach an understanding."

Morton regarded him frostily. "Make your offer."

"Call off your dogs," Hughson said. "I don't know who cracked the safe, and I don't care. What I *do* care about is eliminating Empire Stage Lines. 'Lines!'" he said bitterly. "An old man, a girl, and a snakebit horsebreaker running a couple of broken-down stages."

"For a thousand dollars a mile," Morton smiled.

"A thousand *I* should have. I could give the Post-Office people the kind of service they're paying for. Ask yourself: Is it a kindness to let them bleed to death, instead of giving them a quick and merciful end?"

Sucking a tooth, Morton said, "Seems to me there's a faint odor of death on *you*, my friend. You didn't make much of a fuss when McCool all but announced he'd cuckolded you. When a man won't take up a challenge like that, I begin to wonder how good a man he is."

Hughson stood up. The back of his hand suddenly whipped across Morton's mouth. Morton flinched. He put his fingertips to his lips and glanced at the blood on them. Then he smiled. There was a smear of blood on his teeth.

"You're a pretty good man at that," he said.

"Providing the man you're bucking is small enough. I hope you'll be happy with your new inspector. He'll have a full report on what I think's been happening."

# Chapter Seventeen

AT NINE-THIRTY that night, George Hughson stood in Biff Shackley's quarters and bleakly looked over the dim, liniment-scented room. Shackley had been about as good company as a sand rattler, but he was a single-minded man who knew his job. And he was loyal, something you could not buy. Hughson missed him. He felt as though he had lost his right arm in an accident, and as he began collecting the dead superintendent's belongings in a carton, a deep anger smoldered in his face.

Most of Shackley's possessions had been pocket-knives, tobacco cans, and patent medicines. They filled his chest of drawers and his footlocker. The room would be Artie Judd's now, if he hadn't put his foot in a trap yesterday. Hughson had not seen Judd since they split up at the trail to the caves.

Hughson looked around as someone rode from the alley into the stage yard. He quickly took Shackley's old rifle from the wallpegs, blew out the lamp, and opened the door sufficiently to have a view of the yard. The Mexican hostler was asleep in the feedroom; the other workmen had gone home.

He heard a man softly curse a tired horse as he dismounted. He knew the voice.

"Artie?" he called.

Judd turned and Hughson saw the glint of a revolver. "George?" Judd called back.

"In here." Hughson said.

In Shackley's room, with the door bolted and the lamp relighted, the two men talked. Judd was defensive about the way things had gone.

"Reckon we could have dropped them, but you go to killing women and you're calling out the hornets."

"Nobody's blaming you," Hughson said.

But there was impatience in the way he opened and closed doors, searching for liquor.

"What'd he drink—liniment?" he complained.

He found a half-empty bottle of whiskey and uncorked it. Looking for glasses, he located a tumbler rimmed with alkali and dust. He drank from the neck of the bottle and handed it to Judd. Looking tense and weary, the gunman, drank, then sighed. "Man, man." he said glumly.

"He stayed there. Like you said." Judd added.

"Why didn't you move the gold to another canyon?"

"We moved it to another cave. Spence said Oso

Negro Canyon's the only one with back doors in every direction. How about that fellow Morton? He gonna make us any trouble?"

Hughson took the bottle from Judd's hand, wiped the neck on his shirt and took another pull at the liquor.

"He's not going to make trouble for anybody but himself. He's in Sheriff Murdo's tank. He'll stay there till I give the word to ship him to El Paso."

"How come he's in jail?"

"Bad-check charge," Hughson said. "Now we've got a clear track between us and Empire Stage Lines."

Judd drank again, then sprawled on the cot to peer at the pole-and-mud ceiling. "Now they lay them down and die, eh?"

"Not exactly—we don't have time for a natural death. Tomorrow—next day, maybe—they're sending six hundred dollars to Frontera. We're going to close the books on them, Artie."

"How?"

"On the road somewhere. They can't afford another big loss. You want to move your stuff in here? It'll be your room now."

Still Judd pondered in unhappy silence, and finally Hughson said, "You want to move your stuff in here or not, Artie? What I mean is—I want you to take Shackley's place."

Judd looked surprised. "Me—superintendent?"

"Why not? Anything you need to learn, I'll teach you. After the next few days there won't be any competition, and we can raise prices and start treating ourselves better. Better clothes for you, for instance. You don't have to dress like a hill rancher, like old Biff did. Money in the bank. That's after we clear Empire's plow once and for all."

Judd's simple, gaudy heart was touched. He rolled over on his belly, pulled his gun, and sighted along the barrel at the window.

"Hey, listen! That's my language you're talking."

"Mine, too. Learn your job and I'll make you a junior partner one of these days. I offered old Biff a quarter share a few months ago for a couple of thousand cash, but he couldn't scratch it up. Be thinking about it," he said seriously.

He took a last drink and went out.

The next morning Rian went to the bank.

In his pocket were four checks totaling nearly a thousand dollars, including Potter's check. Bob Moore, the new accountant, had turned up some surprising possibilities in Empire's books—angles which gave them leverage, handles to turn to squeeze money out of reluctant debtors.

The most useful of these tools was the simple device of threatening to sell overdue accounts to an attorney named John Hallon. Hallon specialized in bankruptcy cases. His reputation was such that he usually ate alone in restaurants, but he was a smart and ruthless attorney. Moore told Rian he could siphon all the blood from a man's body with the skill and speed of a six-foot mosquito.

Rian went to Hallon and received his offer of sixty cents on the dollar for all his delinquent accounts.

Then he went around telling the news to the biggest of the accounts, giving them an hour to write a check. When he returned, most of the checks were ready, a hundred cents on the dollar.

He talked to Mr. Noon, the bank manager, a deep-chested hearty old man with a white beard. Noon accepted Rian's deposit, then looked up at him in surprise. They sat by his desk, smoking cigars.

"You've got a talent for collections, Mr. McCool," he said. "I happen to know—well, I won't say I knew they were sweating old Dan Reese down—but they were hoping he'd go broke before they had to pay up. Congratulations."

Rian put the bankbook in his pocket. "Is there a bank in Frontera?" he asked.

"Not yet. We may open one down there ourselves, after we're sure the mines aren't going to play out the way the ones did at Candelaria."

"Then the only way to get money to Texas Mining is to carry the cash?"

Mr. Noon nodded.

Rian frowned and suddenly smiled. "I'll want six hundred of that deposit in gold, then. We'll take it down the river tomorrow."

Noon spoke to a teller, who glanced curiously at Rian and went back to the safe to get the cash. As he was counting out the little piles of double eagles, a stout, red-faced old man in a black suit came to the wicket next to him. Rian heard him say to the teller,

"I want to transfer some funds from my savings account to commercial."

It was the voice of Potter, the feed merchant, whose money now gleamed before Rian in six neat cylinders of gold.

"Six hundred dollars," Rian's teller said briskly.

"And you wanted a sack for it?"

Rian nodded. Uneasily, he glanced at Potter, but the feed merchant seemed not to have heard. Into the sack he dropped the gold pieces. He went out quickly.

Outside the stage office, Dan Reese was soaping hames and looking very gloomy. "Cheer up," Rian told him. "Better times coming."

Inside the station, Bob Moore was poring over the books, clucking over the errors he'd found. Justina gave Rian a wan smile.

"Mr. Moore's making me feel terrible. The things I did were wrong, and the things I didn't do were the things I should have done."

"The thing you should have done," sighed Moore, "was to hire an accountant. I never saw such a set of books."

"They'll look great, once we use up the last of the red ink," Rian told him. He asked Justina, "Have we got a safe?"

"Just a strongbox," said Justina. "I keep it under my bed."

"I want to put something in it," Rian told her.

They went outside.

Justina's father was now burnishing the leather he had soaped. Rian heard him sigh.

"What's on your mind, old timer?" he asked.

Dan raised his head and stared blankly across the yard. "Our driver's quit," he said "I didn't want to tell you."

*"Quit!"*

Dan leaned back against the wall. "Scared out. Too many accidents on our line, he said. Too much going on."

"Where is he?" Rian asked angrily. "I'll either hire him back or make him sorry he ever saw a stagecoach."

"He's done left town," said the old man. Then he looked at his hands, curled his stubby fingers in and stretched them out again.

"Reckon I'll have to go back to driving."

"Oh, Father—!" Justina chided.

"I can drive a coach as well as any of them," Dan stated. "When I married your mother, I was driving three days a week for the old Butterfield line."

"But that was thirty years ago!" The girl looked at Rian, embarrassed by the old man's boasting.

Reese continued working his fingers. "They say a good whip never loses his hands. Let's see if it's true. Anyway, I've played dominoes till I see spots when I close my eyes. Next stage we send up, I'll be driving."

Rian slapped him on the shoulder. "I'll be riding shotgun guard then, and it'll be tomorrow."

The old man's hands dropped to his lap. "Tomorrow! Man alive, I don't know. Tomorrow—!"

"We're taking that money up to Texas Mining. I was thinking: do we have anything but that spavined old Concord stage that will run? Something faster?"

Justina spoke quickly. "We own an old Troy mud wagon. It's under a tarp behind Belder's livery stable. It's light and fast."

"I'll look at it."

He found the ancient Troy coach behind the stable. Pulling the tarp off, he inspected the dusty running gear, and the reach and bolster assembly.

All appeared sound. The customary tooled-leather ornamentation of the Concord coach was heavy duck on the Troy, and the wheels were smaller. But it would do, he decided. Low-slung and fast, it would be a tough wagon to keep up with.

He spoke to the stableman, who agreed to have a couple of men clean the coach up and haul it over to the Empire yard. As he was leaving the stable, a sparkling black turnout with a buckskin mare between the shafts came up the road toward him. He waited for it to pass. When he saw that it was Abby holding the lines, he pushed his hat back and watched her.

She stopped. Smiling, she patted the seat beside her. "I was just looking for someone to talk with," she said.

Rian climbed into the buggy and took the lines from her.

# Chapter Eighteen

"YOU'RE A STUBBORN man, aren't you?" the girl said. They were driving down a narrow road between irrigated fields near the river. Up ahead, a large cottonwood cast a black shadow over the road.

"You know how it is," Rian told her. "Somebody says you can't do it, so you're bound to try."

"You still think you can do it?" In the sunlight, Abby's skin was fine-textured and smooth, rich with warm tones. She had a way of flattering a man with her eyes when she looked at him.

"If I do it," Rian said, "I hope you've got somewhere to jump. Because there won't be much left of Frontera Stage Lines."

"Perhaps I should jump before you do it then. But where?"

Rian looked at her, gazed again at the road and pulled up in the shade of the cottonwood. "There's problems," he admitted.

"I could divorce George, of course," she said, "but then where would I be? Besides, I think you're fond of that Reese girl."

"Just a good friend," Rian said.

He tied the lines and looked into her face. Then he leaned over and pressed his lips against hers. Abby's arms slipped around his neck. After a moment he disengaged himself and took a deep breath.

"Come to think of it," he said, "you're still married, aren't you?"

She pouted. "Is that my fault or yours?"

"I don't know. I've been thinking over what you said about George. You know—dying before his time?"

"And what did you decide?"

"That I'd hate to swing before *my* time. There's a better way. I talked to a lawyer."

"About *me*? You didn't!"

He continued to lie, elaborating on it. "No. About a woman losing her property when she marries, and all that. He said that if a woman took a man to court she might be able to prove that the only reason he married her was for her property. And she'd get it back."

She squeezed his hands. "Really?"

"For a fact."

She pondered it. "But in the meantime he'll lose it all anyway, if you wreck him."

Rian chuckled. "It's hard to know who to back,

isn't it? If you back me—and I lose—you lose, too. But if you stick with George—"

Abby pushed out her lip. "I didn't mean that at all. Would I kiss you this way if I didn't love you?"

She leaned forward, pressed her mouth to his again as she twined her arms about his neck. Rian felt the way he did after a couple of quick shots of whiskey—pleasantly dazed. Then he drove his mind back to Sheriff Crump's jail, in Vallecito. He recalled watching her walk along the street, never looking at him in his cell.

Gently, he disengaged her arms.

"The way we're going," he said, "George is going to get that divorce instead of you."

"Men are so practical," she sighed.

"It's our nature. What might be practical for you would be to slap your husband with a paper and tie up the bank account and all his assets. Then take him to court. I'd win in a walk then."

"Are you sure?"

"Pretty sure. It's worth trying, isn't it?"

"Not if I wreck my husband's line just to save yours so Justina Reese can have you. Is that what you have in mind?"

Rian laughed. "There's the female mind for you! Listen, Abby—Justina may be pretty, but she's not my kind of girl. You're my kind, now that I've broken you to harness."

Abby's lips eased into a smile. "We'd better go back," she said.

Near the village, she said, "It would be better if you got out here."

Rian climbed down.

"I'll speak to George," Abby told him. "I'll tell him what I want: all my property back. If he won't give it to me, I'll move out and start suit."

Abby told George Hughson when he came home for lunch that day. The Mexican girl who cooked for them could not speak English, so Abby told him exactly what she had in mind. Leaning against the jamb of the door, Hughson somberly smoked a cigar while he gazed down the quiet side street on which they lived.

"In other words," he said, "you're asking me for about four thousand dollars cash?"

"Yes. If I've got the cash, I can count on your treating me the way you did before we were married. As long as you know I can move out on you any time I want, you're more likely to show your appreciation of the good wife you have."

Hughson turned. "Were you good in McCool's bed that night?"

Abby's eyes widened. "Who—?"

"McCool was bragging about it," Hughson snapped.

Abby shrugged. "He was lying."

Hughson walked to her. He peered into her face. Then he slapped her, slapped her again, and watched her fall back on the sofa, weeping.

"Pack your things and get out," he said. "You can have your horsebreaker and his bankrupt business. And that's all you ever will have."

He went out and banged the screen door behind him.

Later that afternoon, Potter, the feed man,

entered his office through the side door. Hughson was cool to the man as he lowered his fat backsides onto a chair.

"What's on your mind?" he asked.

Potter lowered his voice. "Anybody around?"

"No."

Potter leaned forward. "I just saw your wife checking into the Mountain View Hotel! Something wrong, George?"

Hughson rocked back in the chair. "Nothing that concerns you, Ira."

"I didn't mean to meddle. Another thing," he said. He glanced into the waiting room, closed that door, and then pulled his chair close to the desk. His watery eyes earnestly sought Hughson's face.

"McCool took six hundred dollars out of the bank this morning!"

"What of it? If you hadn't paid him, he wouldn't have had six hundred to draw out."

"You know why I did it! I was in a terrible bind—"

Hughson scraped under his nails with a gold penknife, saying nothing.

"Now I've got other people on my back," Potter complained. "Everybody I ever owed a dollar to is threatening to take me to court. They figure I'm soft, I suppose—"

"Maybe you are."

Potter sat up in injured dignity. "I paid because I had no choice. If someone's traded sharp with me, they'd better look out or I'll never pay them. There were *rocks* in that river cane I bought from Dan! That's why I let him wait for his money."

Hughson's quiet smile mocked him. Potter was

fearful that he would start buying his feed from someone else. To protect himself he had just appointed himself unofficial informer to Frontera Stages Lines.

"So McCool took out six hundred dollars," Hughson said, finally.

"He asked for a bag to carry the money in! Said it was going on a trip. Just thought you might want to know," Potter said. "Of course it's none of my business. In fact, I'm going to forget I ever heard him, or that I told you."

# Chapter Nineteen

ARTIE JUDD SAUNTERED into the stage yard just before dark. He wore a new lavender shirt in addition to his customary tight, black pants and some yellow dress-boots.

*Now* there *is taste gone wild*! Hughson thought, watching him strut across the yard. The gunman criticized something one of the yard men was doing, halted by a rack of harness bells hung against a wall, and spoke to another man.

"I want these things polished up," Hughson heard him say. "Then hang them inside, out of the weather."

*"Si patrón!"* the Mexican said.

Hughson saw Judd's chest swell. *Sure, boss!* That was the stuff to feed the troops—when they were as vain and stupid as Judd. But for a while

Hughson would have to take the gunman at face value. As Judd sauntered into his office, Hughson exclaimed with pleasure and moved around to look him over with feigned admiration.

"Say! Do you need a note from your mother to buy a shirt like that?"

Judd grinned. "The girls at the Pastime Bar like to tore it off me this noon," he said.

"Wish I could wear colors like that," Hughson flattered him. Then he asked, "Anything doing?"

Judd drew his Colt and spun it by the trigger guard. He gave a short laugh of contempt.

"Old Reese has lost his mind, I reckon. When I went by the stage yard he was setting on a box. He had six pegs driven in the ground with a rein tied to each. He was holding the reins like he was driving a team. He'd say, 'Ho Belle! Ho, Chunk!' and then he'd yank a rein and try to pull the right peg over!"

Hughsons' brow creased. "He used to be a driver before he ranched. Has Simmons quit him?" he asked quickly.

"I don't know."

"If Simmons has quit, he's probably aiming to take his place driving. Artie!" he said suddenly, "that's it! They're sending money to Frontera tomorrow. It's dollars to washers Dan Reese will be driving."

Excitement came up full and strong in him. He sat behind his desk, spun a scratch pad before him and picked up a pencil. "Come here," he said. Judd came around the desk as Hughson sketched a map.

"Know where the road skirts Cerro Colorado?"

Judd leaned on the desk by one hand. "Reckon so," he said dubiously.

"You'd better know so before you leave town tonight."

"Didn't know I was leaving."

"You're leaving as soon as it's dark." Hughson turned the map so that Judd could see it, his pencil point tracing the stage road. "Cerro Colorado's that red slide south of the road. The road climbs across the foot of it. The rocks are as big as horse troughs, and loose. They used to have slides there all the time. Do you remember the place?" he asked intently.

Judd scratched his neck. "I know it. But—"

"It wouldn't take much to start another slide, Artie. Just one shot of blasting powder."

Judd shook his head. "All I know about blasting powder you could heap on a beer check."

Scowling, Hughson weighed the odds. It was too good a chance to pass up. Yet he did not dare to be on the ground himself when it happened. Even old Marshal Fowley might get curious about a coincidence like that if anyone saw him in the area.

He explained how simple it was to set a couple of sticks of explosive in place. He figured how much fuse Judd should attach to the cap.

"I'll give you two feet of red-dot fuse. Light it as soon as the coach comes past the dead tree I've marked—right here. I've timed it all out before— just in case," he said. "Or, if you're a good rifle shot, you can leave the cap exposed and put a shot into it from a distance."

"I can't hit the backside of a bull from fifty feet," Judd frowned.

"Then use the fuse. Their regular stage leaves here at one p.m. They've got a watering-and-rest stop a mile or two short of the slide. So they'll be going more or less full-bore at the slide."

Judd's thick features still seemed unhappy as he studied the map.

"All you have to do afterwards," Hughson said, "is turn your horse around and come back. Take the river trail and you won't be seen. And then we're in business!" he finished, clapping the gunman on the shoulder.

Judd folded the map and slipped it in the pocket of his new lavender shirt. His small eyes gazed into the stage man's for a moment. Then he nodded.

"Where's the stuff?"

All afternoon Justina had behaved very coolly toward Rian. At first he thought she was merely preoccupied. But when, that evening, he said, "I think we ought to hide that cash under your bed now," she retorted, "I don't care what you do with it. Why don't you buy Mrs. Hughson some matched blacks for her town buggy?"

She marched out of the office, banging the door after her. Rian stared after her as she hurried in the darkness toward the living quarters. Baffled, he gazed at Bob Moore.

"What ails the female, Bob?"

"Just that, I reckon," the old man said. "Bein' a crazy female."

"She's been a female as long as I've known her,"

Rian said, "but she hasn't acted like this before."

*Except*, he recalled, *when she found Abby'd been to see me at the hotel.*

*Great snakes!* he thought. *Did she see me in Abby's buggy this morning?*

He strode after her. In the darkness, he heard the screen door bang closed. A moment later he opened the door. She was not in sight, but he saw a lamp come on in the kitchen. She had placed it in a wall bracket and was tying the strings of an apron behind her as he came into the doorway.

"Hey!" he called.

Justina banged open the draft on the small iron cookstove and removed the lids in order to start a fire. She paid him no attention at all.

"What did you mean about Mrs. Hughson's buggy?" he asked.

Still she did not answer. She stuffed newspapers into the firebox, took three pieces of kindling from the woodbox and arranged them atop the paper. Rian crossed the tiny room and touched her arm.

Justina whirled and slapped him.

Then she covered her face with her hands and began to weep. Rian pulled her hands down, chuckling. "You saw us, didn't you?"

The girl turned her face from him. "Go away! The whole thing was a plan to wreck us, wasn't it? You're just doing what she tells you to."

"No! It was business. She's trying to use me, see? So I decided to let her try. And at the same time, I'm using her."

"How?"

He told her.

"Now she's moving out on Hughson. If she starts suit to recover her property, it'll tie him up legally so he can't even sign a mail contract. She may be able to attach his assets while they fight the suit. Isn't that worth taking a buggy ride for?"

Justina sniffled. "I suppose . . ."

The screen door creaked open and there was an apologetic tap. "Miss Justina?" called Bob Moore.

Justina pulled her apron up and wiped her nose and eyes. "Yes?" she called.

"A lady to buy a ticket," Moore said. "Afraid I don't know how to write it up."

"Oh. Well, I'll do it. Just a minute! Do you know the lady?"

Rian, too, thought it curious that Moore would not say who the lady was, in a town of that size. It was an event of local importance when anyone crossed the street.

"Yes, ma'am. It's Mrs. Hughson," Moore called back.

They looked at one another. Rian grinned. "You see? She's walking out on him!"

Justina put her hands to her cheeks. "Do you really think—?"

"Go sell that ticket," Rian said. "Best if I stay out of sight."

After Justina left the house, Rian sat on the worn plush sofa. *A week ago*, he reflected, *I was sitting in a jail cell with no women at all. Now I've got a choice of two. Of course it was no choice, really. Picking Abby would be like picking a side winder. The longest day of her life, she would remember that when she wrote for him to come to her, he never answered the letter.*

He went into the kitchen and completed the fire Justina had been building. Lighting it, he replaced the black iron lids and adjusted the draft and damper. He filled the hot-water reservoir and started some coffee.

Justina came back, her eyes sparkling. "It's true! She's going to Frontera tomorrow. Do you really think that's what she's going to do?"

"Let's wait and see. Where's Dan?"

"He's been in the harness room most of the afternoon, tending the reins he's going to use. Soap, conditioner—it's ridiculous, you'd think he was getting married or something."

"It'll be good for him," Rian said. "And look at the money we'll save. Later on we can hire another driver and add service to Fort Biggs, with Dan holding down the Frontera stage."

Justina smiled. "You don't have to be a dreamer to be a stage man," she said, "but it certainly helps."

# Chapter Twenty

ARTIE JUDD SPENT the night on Cerro Colorado.

From the top of the hill, broad and flat like an old cinder cone, he could gaze down on the shallow valley the stage road traversed on its way to Frontera. Far out in the hills he could see a few lights, like cigarette sparks, where small ranchers had their homes.

The slope climbed steeply from the stage road, a great talus of porous red blocks of volcanic stone. They seemed so precariously balanced that he postponed finding a spot for the dynamite until morning. He had the feeling that if you loosened exactly the right boulder, the little valley would be brimful of rocks a minute later.

That night he made his camp just back from the top of the slide. The old crater was filled to the brim with fine sand deposited there by the windstorms that frequently howled through this country.

Judd scooped out a hollow and built a little fire with deadfall from some alligator junipers growing on the slope. He had nothing to cook, but the fire melted the loneliness around him until he was ready to sleep.

In the morning he looked over the ground carefully, back door and front.

The back door was the bosque of the river. To use it, he would have to follow the perimeter of the cinder cone and ride down the back way into the bosque. On that side of the hill the ground was much more even. It slid out to the river right where Santa Cruz Canyon opened like a door for the river to enter.

In the clear, winey light of dawn, the gunman scrutinized the valley before him.

In the bottom, the volcanic stone had decomposed sufficiently to be called earth. There were a few cottonwoods and junipers through which the stage road took a reasonably straight path. Judd picked out the dead tree Hughson had mentioned. A quarter of a mile south of the tree, the road passed under a ledge of tumbled red boulders.

*That's the spot he meant*, Judd decided.

He spent another ten minutes satisfying himself that there was no one on the road; that no Mexican goat-herds were in the area, no cowboys poking around hunting stray cows. Then he picked his way down the slope with the dynamite, caps, and fuse shoved into his shirt. Once, a boulder shifted under his boot and he had to jump. Cursing, he fingered the dynamite and wondered what would happen if he fell on it.

Picking his spot with care, he tucked the two sticks of explosive under a rock and affixed the cap. Then he stretched the fuse out so that one portion of it could not ignite another portion with its sparks and cause a premature explosion.

He stood up and considered the whole scene. He envisioned the boulder jarring lazily a couple of feet into the air, coming down upon the stones below it, as the whole mass began to move.

It took him a minute and a half to regain the summit. He looked at his watch again; it was nine-fifteen. He stretched out on his back in the floury-fine sand and gazed up at some buzzards revolving on the rim of an invisible wheel.

Dan Reese spent most of the morning sitting on the box of the old Troy coach, getting the feel of it. Every time Rian passed, the old man would call to him.

"It's a great feeling, boy!" he said once. "You're the king of the mountain up here. All them horses working for you! You can make any one of them sit down and slide or stretch his neck, just by bending your finger!"

"See to it you bend the right finger," Rian suggested. He hoped the old man still had his stage man's hands, if he'd ever had them.

A boy from the hotel came to the stage depot at eleven-thirty with two large suitcases of Abby

Hughson's. Rian stowed them inside the luggage boot. At twelve, Abby came and settled herself in the waiting room. Rian avoided going into the station.

A few minutes later old Potter showed up. He had a half-filled gunnysack slung over his shoulder. Stiff and red-faced, he stared at Rian, who was helping Dan tar axles on the Troy. He shook up the sack.

"I want to send this to Frontera," he said.

"What is it?"

"Feed sample. Not exactly to Frontera—to a farmer near there. You can drop it by the road at Tolson's turnoff."

Reese started a hub nut back onto the threads. "Take it into the office. My clerk will give you a tag to make out. The old busybody," he muttered, as Potter trudged into the office. "He likely saw Mrs. Hughson coming here. He just wants to make sure before he tells on her. Feed samples!"

When Potter left, he walked at his customary dignified gait to the corner, then broke into an uneven hurrying stride. Panting, he walked into the stage yard and hurried to Hughson's side door. Without knocking, he opened it and went inside.

The stage man was not there.

Potter groaned. He was just turning away when Hughson came in, big, square-shouldered, somberly dressed. Hughson drove a glance of displeasure into Potter's eyes, saw something he had not expected there, and frowned.

"What's the matter?"

"Maybe nothing, George. Only—well, did you know Mrs. Hughson's going down to Frontera on that stage today?"

It hit Hughson with blinding force. He put out a hand to steady himself as his heart squeezed down, then exploded into violent pumping.

"How do you know?" he asked.

"She's in their waiting room right now!"

Hughson realized something about himself he had not been aware of. He still loved Abby; had somehow thought he'd make her come back, but on his terms. The magnitude of the threatening disaster overwhelmed him.

After a moment he managed to recover his self-possession. He jingled some coins in his pockets. "All right. Thanks for telling me," he said.

"I thought I'd better let you know."

"Thanks. I may speak to her, may not. Pretty hard to change a woman's mind, eh? Married men like you should know that, Ira."

Potter gave a flabby grin, chuckled, and went to the door. "Well, just thought I'd—good-bye," he said.

Hughson sank into the chair.

Now what?

Run down to the station and tell Abby that she mustn't take that stage, because it was going to be obliterated from the face of the earth? Put a weapon like *that* in her hands?

God, no!

On the other hand—let her ride into the trap with the others? He put his fingertips to his temples and massaged them. He glanced at the clock. Twelve-fifteen. Forty-five minutes before the stage left.

Anything he did involving Abby was going to be noticed, and when the stage was wrecked the finger would instantly point at him. He could not forcibly drag her home, argue with her, or try to delay the stage. Anything he did would incriminate him later.

Forty-five minutes. Time to ride up and call off the show for today? A stage traveled faster than a rider, but he would have nearly an hour's head start if he left at once. He could take short cuts across the hills and through the gullies. He would have to rest his horse frequently, but so would the stage team have to rest, since it was a two-bit outfit with no way station where a fresh team was backed onto the pole.

At last it came to him that this was the only thing he could do: ride like the devil to Cerro Colorado. If he made it in time, well and good. If he was late, he would still have a small lead on the stage. He could find a good vantage point near the road and drop one of the horses with a rifle shot. That would slow the stage enough so that the blast would go off prematurely.

A rifle. He had several, but all were at home, a fifteen-minute ride. Then he remembered that Shackley's old rifle was still in his room. Such as it was, it would have to do.

He walked to the barn and found a hostler. "Saddle my grulla," he told the man.

"Yes, sir." But the stableman hesitated. "The grulla? You don't ride him much, Mr. Hughson. He's full of beans. Likely act up a bit."

"That's why I want the grulla. He needs to be ridden more often. He's a good, strong animal, but he needs to know who's boss."

"Yes, sir."

Hughson sauntered to Shackley's room, un-locked it and went inside. Quickly, he lifted the rifle from its wall pegs. It weighed about fifteen pounds, solid bronze, and looked as though Shackley's grandfather might have carried it in the War of 1812. However, it was a Colt revolving six-shot, with a loading lever fitting under the octagonal barrel. He cocked it and peered down the barrel. He could see light through the fire hole and knew it was unloaded.

Searching quickly through Shackley's effects, he found a box of linen cartridges. He put one in each chamber, rammed it home, pinched priming caps onto the nipples, and looked for rifle balls. Finally he found a quantity of them in the hollow stock of the gun. He inserted the first ball and worked the loading lever again; immediately the ball rolled out.

*My God!* he thought bitterly. *An old paper-patch model!*

He tore a few postage stamp-size patches from a newspaper. After laying a patch over the chamber, he pressed the ball home with his thumb, then rammed it in place. This time it stayed in the gun. He finished loading and went outside.

He carried the rifle to the alley, holding it parallel to his body so that it might not be noticed. He walked a few yards down the alley and leaned the gun against the back of a building.

When the horse was ready, he told the hostler, "I may not come back after lunch. I've got some papers to work on at home."

He rode down the alley, picked up the gun, and

cut through a vacant lot southwest toward the river road. As soon as he was on the road, he put the horse into an easy lope, riding well forward over the withers to ease the load on the animal's back. The horse would never be worth a damn after today but, by Heaven, it would have to make it to the slide in time!

# Chapter Twenty-One

FIVE MINUTES BEFORE stage time, Rian carried the express box from the station. Within its battered oaken shell was the dark gleam of six hundred dollars in gold, plus a few things consigned to the post office in Frontera. The box was shoved far under the driver's seat, the mail sack jammed in on top of it. The six-horse team, held by a couple of hostlers, was already in the traces.

At stage time, Dan Reese swaggered from the house, pulling on new buckskin gauntlets as yellow as wildflowers.

Standing with Rian, Justina whispered, "Pray Heaven he's up to it! So far, I think it's just a game with him. How can a man handle a six-horse team after so long?"

As the old man prepared to mount, Rian had an impulse to help him. He suppressed it. If Dan couldn't mount the box, then, by George, he wasn't ready to drive! But Dan climbed easily to the deck, took up the lines and began separating them.

"Bo-*ard*!" Rian bawled.

Abby appeared in the depot door. Across the tawny ground she smiled at him. She waited an instant, as if hoping he would come to offer his arm. Instead, he tossed his rifle to the deck, smiled good-bye to Justina, and waited by the door of the coach.

Abby came forward. He marveled at how well she carried off the delicate situation. Still, she'd always been able to fake the part of the fine lady. Hard to believe that a few days ago the fine lady was suggesting he kill her husband for her!

Small, perfumed, and meticulously turned out in a gray and blue traveling dress, she stood before him.

"Are we all ready to leave?" she asked. "I hate to board until stage time."

"All ready, ma'am," he said with mock dignity. "That's what I was yelling about." He took her elbow and helped her into the coach. "Curtains up or down?" he asked.

"Up please," she said, smiling.

Once she was settled—the only passenger—he closed the door. He rolled up the canvas curtains and secured them. He climbed to the box and put his rifle across his knees.

"All set, Dan," he said.

The first two miles were the hardest. For a while Rian had to close his eyes. Dan was overdriving, the horses cutting this way and that as his messages traveled down the lines in a series of nervous tugs. Once a leader stumbled and there was a near pile-up.

But that somehow relaxed the old man.

He began to settle down. He even glanced at Rian with a faint grin.

"Relax, young fellow," he said over the ringing clatter of hoofs and wheels. "I got the feel of it now."

"And not a minute too soon," Rian said. "We were about to get the feel of the rocks by the road."

Judd looked at his watch every few minutes. Sometimes, when he looked, only a minute would have passed. He was nerved up like a bride. He laid out some matches for the fuse, then put them away. He was afraid they might be ignited accidentally and set fire to the fuse. He lay only a few feet from it.

His vantage point was two-thirds of the way down the slope. He could see as far as the dead tree by the road—the key to the whole attack. Judd's mouth was dry. In his hip pocket was a bottle of whiskey, half emptied during the night by his campfire. He took it out, uncorked it, then shoved the cork into the neck again, returning it to his pocket. Later.

There was damned little fire left in Hughson's grulla now. High on grain and barn sour, it had soaked up a lot of spurring before the work of carrying the big man on its back settled it down. Now its tawny sides were black with sweat, its nostrils flared.

Hughson pulled up on a lift of ground and looked at his watch. Two-forty! He figured the stage would pass Cerro Colorado at three. Give or take ten minutes, Judd would have to be a clumsier man than Hughson surmised him to be to fail in his job. The slide, once started, should spread over a hundred feet.

Scrutinizing his back trail, he saw a ragged feather of dust against the desert. Hughson groaned. It had to be the coach. He spurred the horse hard, studying the red hill a few miles ahead. To be safe, he took a route paralleling the road but a few hundred yards to the right of it. Thus, if he had to, he would be in position to shoot one of the lead horses and stop the stage.

Two miles from Cerro Colorado, Dan Reese stopped the stage to rest the horses. He got down and walked around to test the tugs and traces. "They're really working," he called up to Rian. "Hitting the collars all together. Next time I'll latch 'em up looser—give 'em more freedom to move."

Rian leaned overside. "Everything all right, ma'am?" he called to Abby.

The girl was patting dust from her face with a kerchief. "Would you mind putting down the curtains now?" she asked.

"My pleasure," Rian said.

By the time he had finished lowering and tying the curtains, the horses had stopped blowing. "We'd best be rolling," said Dan. "Don't want them stiffening up."

Rian stood on the deck a moment to study the

ground. He looked over the long, red slide ahead for the flash of metal or for movement. But there was no sign of trouble, and if anybody tried to stop them he had a rifle filled with bullets as big as his thumb to discourage them.

"Okay," he said, sitting down. "Let's roll."

Dan Reese kicked off the brake, and with a squeal of bull-hide thorough braces, the old Troy rolled on down the road.

When it passed a dead alligator-juniper beside the road, the horses tossed their head and shied. Good sign, Rian thought, the foolish animals were feeling good. Old Dan still had his stage man's hands.

Then something happened that dynamited the quiet afternoon apart like an artillery shell.

The right lead-horse suddenly threw itself against its mate. At the same time it uttered a scream that made the goose flesh rise on Rian's arms. Distinctly, he heard a loud *pop*. Then he saw the blood spurting from its right shoulder.

The horse fell, and in an instant the rest of the team had piled up in a hopeless knot of squealing animals, kicking legs, and tangled harness. Rian crouched on the deck and looked for the sniper, as he heard a rifle shot echoing back and forth down the slope at the right of the road.

"What the devil?" Dan shouted. "Rian, what did I do? What happened?"

"Pile off!" Rian shouted. "Get behind the coach. We're under fire."

Dan scrambled to the road, lugging Justina's little buggy rifle, Rian sprawling after him. Inside the buggy, he heard Abby scream. The door opened on the far side and she stepped down. She ran past the threshing, bellowing team and stopped in the center of the road with her hands over her ears.

"Get down!" Rian shouted. "Take cover."

Abby stared wildly at the team, then at Rian; he had the feeling that nothing registered with her. Dust exploded in the road between her and the team. Then they heard the violent echoes of another rifle shot. She screamed, took a few running steps, caught her foot in her skirt, and fell. Still screaming, she got to her feet and started on.

Rian ran after her. "Come back here, you little idiot!"

He would not have believed it was possible to run so fast in skirts. Holding her skirts knee-high, the girl ran down the sandy crown of the road.

Something passed Rian with a sound like tearing linen.

A bullet struck a rock on the far side of the road and caromed off. Rian threw himself to the ground. Sprawled there like an infantryman, he searched for the source of the shot.

High among the rocks he saw a smear of powder smoke. He aimed the old Springfield with care and squeezed off a shot. Dust sprang up where it struck. He fired again, dazed by the suddenness with which disaster had come. Abby was still running, and now he realized there was no logic in following her; he was the target, not she.

He waited an instant, gathered himself and sprinted back to the coach at a staggering run. Dan was trying to cut the dead animal out of the traces to get the others back on their feet.

"Leave him!" Rian shouted, seizing him by the shoulder and dragging him into the shelter of the coach.

"They're sufferin'," Dan protested, bewildered.

"Better them suffering than us dying," Rian panted. "Stay down and look for targets."

# Chapter Twenty-Two

A HALF MINUTE passed.

Rian saw movement in the boulders along the rim of the red hill. He took aim, but before he could fire, a man had risen quickly, taking a few running steps and vanishing over the crest.

Then he felt a massive jolt in the earth, a tremor which was followed by a puff of wind against his face. Motion in the slide farther up the road drew his gaze. He stared.

"Dan—look!" he gasped.

A great mass of boulders was rising from the earth on a mushrooming column of dust; smaller stones soared high, twisting and turning in the air. As the larger rocks fell back, a slide started. In a dusty tangle of brush and small junipers, the boulders plunged downhill toward the road. The rumble of their movement came through the earth.

Rian came slowly to his feet, a coldness spreading through him. He saw Abby standing beside the road, facing the slide. She began to run. As she ran, the path of the rock slide widened. A few smaller stones bounded down the slope and landed near the road. Abby swerved, leaving the road to run across the narrow valley between the hills. She stumbled and fell, regained her feet and ran a little farther before a sotol cactus tangled her skirts and stopped her.

As she tried to pull free, the base of the slide stirred with a bass grunting sound. Here and there, puffs of dust burst from it. The mass began to settle almost wearily, seeking its own level. Already littered with smaller stones, the road now began to be covered with larger ones. Then there was a louder roar, a muted thunder, as the slide spread.

"Mother of God!" Dan whispered.

Small rocks were landing near Abby. Leaving half her dress tangled in the cactus, she pulled free. A few stones were landing beyond her now. And, as they watched, the road itself was engulfed by the rockslide. A hole had been scooped out where the explosion tore the first boulders away. Now the rocks above the hole loosened and crashed into it, and after that the slide seemed to flow like a river of mud, covering the road, spilling across it onto the level ground, burying everything in its path.

At last there was an aching stillness.

The valley boiled with dust. A few more boulders

broke loose and bounded down the slope. Rian
could not see the place where Abby had vanished.
He was not anxious to. Trembling, he turned to the
old man.

"Let's get these horses straightened out before
they kill themselves," he said.

Four of the horses were uninjured, but one was
dead of the gunshot which had dropped it, and
another had a broken foreleg. They destroyed it,
then led the others to nearby trees where they
tethered them. They rolled the Troy off the road,
and Rian unearthed the mail sack and express box
and hid them in some brush.

"It's funny," Dan said. "Them shooting that
horse. If they were going to wipe us out anyway,
why fire at the horse and stop the stage?"

"I reckon that's it, Dan," he said. "Somebody
*was* trying to stop it. He stopped us, but he couldn't
stop Abby. I'm going to look around," he said.

"I'll go along."

Rian started to tell him to stay with the horses,
but decided the old man was probably equal to a
little more excitement, and he needed his gun, puny
as it might be.

"Let's work around back of the hill," he said.
"Take us an hour to hike up the slide. And I've kind
of lost my appetite for rock climbing anyway."

They walked west a quarter of a mile, then turned
south toward the river road which Rian and Justina
had followed the other day. Just before they reached
the road, Rian put out a hand to halt Dan.

Two horsemen had reined up in the trail a couple

of hundred yards ahead. Both men instantly brought rifles to their shoulders, and Rian and Dan hit the ground.

Hughson swore as he spurred his horse into a tangle of mesquite, seeing the men in the trail. Artie Judd was right behind him, and just as they entered the brush a couple of bullets ripped through the branches. The booming thunder of a Springfield rolled down the bosque, followed by the thin crack of a lighter rifle.

Judd was afire with excitement. "Let's run over them!" he said, "Roust 'em out and gun 'em down."

"Use your head," Hughson said. "We couldn't hit them at a run. They'd knock us out of the saddle. We're going down to Oso Negro Canyon and pick up Spence and that cash."

He was talking fast but hearing the words as though someone else were speaking them. Something told him to keep going; that the only chance to avoid being overwhelmed by what he had just seen was to drive ahead.

"We'll be in a box, George," Judd argued.

We're in a box now. I didn't count on survivors. We've got to bring Spence out, and we're liable to need that money he's sitting on. McCool will follow us in. If three of us can't whip him and old Reese, we're finished anyway."

He dismounted and crawled to a spot from which he could see the back trail. Then he raised his gun and fired one of his remaining shots at the place where he had last seen the stage men. He sprang up.

"Let's go!"

Staying in the thickets, they entered Santa Cruz Canyon, then pulled into the trail and loped down the river. In ten minutes they reached the confluence of Oso Negro Canyon and rode up this side canyon toward the cave.

When they reached it, Spence called from a ledge above the cave where he had been lying in ambush. "I thought you'd done forgot me! I've had nothing to eat but soda crackers since yesterday."

"Stick with me, Spence," Hughson retorted, "and you'll be eating bullets before nightfall. Where's the money?"

Bewildered, the fox-faced man jumped to a lower ledge and slid to the base of the slope. "Buried in the cave," he said. And seeing Hughson's face, he asked, "What's up?"

"I'll tell you while we dig it up. I want it stowed on my saddle and the horse hidden farther up."

The sun had fallen deeply behind the rimrock above the river. Rian and Dan Reese reached the confluence of Oso Negro Canyon and scrutinized the narrow, brushy passage between the cliffs.

Remembering his experience of the other day, Rian did not intend to be trapped again. He banked on Judd and Hughson's heading up Oso Negro. There was little chance of overtaking them without horses, but there were places in this country where a horse could not go. Perhaps, if crowded hard enough, they would blunder into one of those blind alleys.

Rian chose the south side of the canyon for himself. He told Dan:

"Work up about fifty feet from the floor but stay in the brush. Don't try to move too fast. If we're fired at, dig in and wait. Let them make the mistakes."

As Dan climbed the north slope, he picked his own way through brush and broken stone to a faint cattle trail on the opposite wall. When they were both in position, he made a signal to start working up the canyon. In this fashion they advanced a half mile. The light was already failing.

The first indication that they had made contact came as a shattering volley of gunfire and blasting echoes.

He hit the ground. Across the canyon he heard Dan fire back. After a moment he raised his head and tried to see movement. No one stirred, but he saw a thin curl of smoke from a thicket. Someone had been having a smoke while he waited. Across his rifle sights, Rian watched. The light struck a spark from a spur; then he made out the shape of a man's boot. Finally he discerned the gunman huddled in the brush. It was too dark to draw decent aim. Rian found a chunk of chalky stone and rubbed his sights. Into the white pattern of sights, he set his target.

He tightened his trigger finger slowly. The shot jarred his shoulder.

With a cry, a man rose from the brush and stumbled into the trail. It looked like Judd. He fell and went sprawling down the steep slope into the thickets.

Another volley of firing came from a well-screened point farther on. Dan sent a small-caliber bullet into the brush. Lying low, Rian waited a moment, then fired back. He had little hope of hitting anything. Yet he dared not try to close in until it was darker. And by then the others would be taking advantage of the darkness to escape. Bitterly, he settled down to wait.

# Chapter Twenty-Three

HUGHSON WISHED HE could recover Judd's rifle. It was an old Henry that held fifteen shots. This cannon of Shackley's, while it was a six-shot, was a bear cat to load. Now the cylinder was empty, darkness was gathering, and he wanted a full magazine before they headed for the horses.

Spence went on guard while he reloaded. Down at the foot of the slope lay the sprawled shape of Judd. Hughson felt no regret there; he had been paying for his gun, not his appetites, and from now on Judd would have been a harder man to handle.

Hughson crammed the loads into the gun and counted six balls from the gunstock. Remembering that he needed patches to make the bullets stay in, he searched his pockets for scraps of paper. There was nothing. His hand closed on his buckskin money purse. In addition to some gold coins, it contained a thin fold of goldbacks. Reluctantly, he peeled off a five-dollar bill and tore it lengthwise, tore it again into four strips an inch wide. He ripped one of the strips into postage stamp-sized patches and completed the job of loading.

From time to time McCool and the old man would open on the cave with a blasting volley that shook the canyon. When they did so, Spence and Hughson would wait, then return the fire as soon as it slackened.

Hughson had to reload once again. At last it was dark; time to try to get out of the trap.

"Spence!" he called.

There was no reply from the gunman.

"Spence!"

Still no answer, and Hughson crawled from the cave to where he lay. When he touched him, Spence did not move. Hughson's hand drew back quickly. He knew, then, that he had been alone for some time. Spence was dead.

He rose to a crouch and headed up the canyon, moving clumsily, with a feeling of panic. He hoped the horse was still tethered in the clump of desert cedar where he had left it. God help him if it was gone!

But when he reached the spot, the horse was still there, soaped with sweat. He tightened the cinches, threw off the tether, and mounted. As the horse started to climb the rimrock to the crest, gunfire broke out far below him. Hughson did not quicken his gait; only a freak shot could stop him now.

Reaching the summit, he swung east toward the stage road.

Rian struck a match and gazed around the deep, low-ceilinged cave. He and Dan had found the two dead men outside it. Until the last moment, Rian had hoped one of them would be Hughson. But the man was gone; gone with three thousand dollars; gone with his guilt and perhaps even a sick conscience for the wife he had killed.

By all the evidence, Spence had been living in the cave for several days. There were empty cans, a sack of soda crackers, and dozens of wheat-straw cigarette butts. A pack of greasy cards was laid out in a half-finished game of solitaire.

But there was no money, and nothing incriminating. Then Rian noticed some scraps of paper on the floor.

"What's this—confetti?" he said. He gathered up a half dozen scraps of paper.

By matchlight, they inspected the bits of paper and found them to be a torn-up goldback. "Save 'em," the old man said. "If there's more'n half of a bill, the bank will give you five dollars."

Rian's brow wrinkled. "I'd give ten to know why somebody tore this up." He tucked the pieces into his shirt pocket. "Funny..."

The old man sprawled back against the sloping wall. "Man, man, I am so tired!" he sighed. "I ain't walked that far in twenty years."

"Or been shot at so much?"

"Or been shot at. Not since the war. Did you know I was in the First Illinois, McCool? I was a corporal at first, but in only four years I rose to sergeant. If the war'd lasted, I mighta made warrant officer."

He laughed, and Rian chuckled. "I like your spirit, Dan. I may put you on steady."

"Son, I wouldn't go back to dominoes for anything! I was going into dry rot there. Terrible. Only thing is—have we got a stage line now?"

Rian sprawled on his back, resting. "Why not? We've got a franchise and enough horses to pull the Troy."

"But we haven't got any money," the old man said.

"Maybe that goldback will buy us everything we need, Dan," Rian said thoughtfully.

"What do you mean?"

"Just surmising. Wake me up in about a half-hour, will you? I've got a long walk back tonight."

"Tonight! Reckoned we'd rest tonight and go back tomorrow."

"I want to get back as soon as I can. Likely be dawn before I make it to Kingbolt. I want you to find a nice clean cave and catch yourself a snooze. Tomorrow I'll pick you up beside the road. Okay?"

"Okay. Half-hour?"

Rian nodded. In a few moments he was asleep. Almost immediately the old man was shaking his shoulder.

"'Bout that time, son. Sure you want to start back tonight?"

Rian sighed. "Got to, Dan."

"Here's some so-so coffee. I found some cake

coffee and mixed it with hot water. It'll speed you on your way."

After Rian had drunk the coffee, he told the old man to take care of himself, and hiked down the trail toward the main canyon.

About nine o'clock he reached the stage road. He checked the horses before moving on. Chunk, the best of their lead animals, gave him a friendly nudge as he unwound the rope the horse had wrapped around the tree with his nervous stompings.

He looked the horse over thoughtfully, wondering if it had ever carried a rider. Probably not. But a tractable horse could be talked into all sorts of things. And that was a brutally long walk for a man who was tired and sick with killing and seeing murder done.

He fashioned a hackamore from a rope, and the horse accepted it. Then he led it out to the road and tried throwing a leg across the horse and sliding back, doing this repeatedly until at last it let him sit astraddle. This horse, he decided, had carried a man before. It was the kind of horse the Reeses would have had to take as second choice, rather than the strong lively animal a stage man would ordinarily pick.

At a ragged jog, he started for Kingbolt...

The town looked dead when he rode up the main street. Before the saloons, where few horses were tethered, some men talked quietly. All the other buildings were dark, except for an occasional night lamp. A cat scurried across the street; somewhere beyond town a pack of coyotes yelped.

There was still a light in Marshal Fowley's office.

Rian tied the big horse and stretched. The broad back of the animal had nearly split him like a wedge. Lugging the rifle, he went to the door and glanced inside. He heard Fowley's voice in the hall leading to his cells.

"I'm not going to fool around with you no more, Billy. I don't mind a man getting tanked up now and then and riding his horse down the walks. But this business of challenging everybody in town to do battle, after two drinks! Either you cut it out or I'll send you over to Huntsville next time."

A drunken voice said, "Mize well make up my ticket, Marshal. I got this town in my pocket—"

Fowley came in, muttering under his breath, and saw Rian standing in his office. Fowley needed a shave, and he looked half spent. Seeing Rian, his manner sharpened quickly.

"Am I glad to see you!" he said.

"What's happened?" Dead tired, Rian leaned against the wall.

"Thought you were going to tell *me* what's happened. A goatherder came in town tonight and told me there'd been a big rockslide at Cerro Colorado. I got to thinking—"

"It missed us," Rian said.

He told him the story.

"What makes you so sure it was Hughson?" the marshal asked, finally.

"I saw him and found the bodies of two of his men. Do you need any more proof than that?"

Fowley nodded. "Certainly I do. You saw him at

a distance of a hundred feet—right? It could have been anybody. Mind you, I don't doubt your story. I'm just telling you what we'd be up against if we took him to court with no more evidence than that."

Rian drew his hand from his pocket. He dropped on the desk several of the scraps of paper he had found in the cave. "How about these?" he asked. "I found them in the hideout."

Fowley moved them around with a fingertip, studying them. "What are they?"

"Let's ask Hughson."

Sweeping the scraps into his palm, Fowley said, "All right. We'll talk to him."

Because Hughson's office was closer, they looked at the depot first. The door was unlocked and a lamp was burning on the desk, but Hughson was not in the room.

"He must be around," Fowley muttered. "Wouldn't go off and leave the place unlocked."

Through the dusty panes of Biff Shackley's room, they saw the stage man stretched out on the cot with his arm covering his face. A bottle rested on the floor beside him and his rifle was tilted against the wall.

Fowley moved to the door and turned the porcelain knob. Through the window, Rian saw Hughson quickly swing his legs over the side of the cot and reach for the rifle. Rian leveled his revolver at the man, waiting as Fowley went in.

Hughson, dazed with fatigue, managed to smile. "Oh—it's you, Marshal."

"Just checking around, George," said the marshal. "Your office was unlocked."

Hughson scrubbed his face with his hands. "Sorry," he muttered.

The marshal glanced about the room. "Sleeping down here now, George?"

"Just resting. I went home at noon and didn't come back until after closing time. Marshal," he said, "my wife's left me."

"That's too bad," said Fowley. He was still looking the room over, seemingly paying no attention to Hughson. But now he opened his hand and showed the stage man the bits of torn paper. "Know anything about these, George?"

Rian came into the doorway. Hughson did not immediately see him. Apparently stunned, he gazed at the scraps.

"No. I don't. What are they?"

At the same time, he moved toward his rifle. But what he picked up was the pint bottle of liquor. He took a small, careful drink and lowered the bottle.

The marshal glanced at Rian. "Frankly, I don't know. Want to tell him what you think they are?" he asked Rian.

Hughson's eyes drilled at Rian's face. "Take the rifle," Rian told the marshal. "Pull one of the loads and see what he used for a patch. *I* think he got caught short in that cave and used a torn-up goldback."

Marshal Fowley moved nearer the cot and picked up the rifle. Hughson made no move until the marshal began examining the cylinder. Then, in two swift motions, he hurled the bottle at Rian and smashed the lamp from the wall above the bed. In an instant the room was dark.

Hughson fired. Rian dropped to his knees. The concussion of the shot hit his body like a fist, as his ears went dead. But in the flash he saw Hughson lying on the floor with a revolver in his hand. He had fired high, at the place where Rian had stood an instant before.

Rian snapped a shot back at him. In the gun flash, he saw the marshal swinging the rifle to cover Hughson; an instant later it roared. Hughson groaned. Rian fired again, then lunged toward the man and seized his gun. Hughson's slack hand released it. He moaned as Rian pulled away.

"McCool?" the marshal asked sharply.

"Right here. He's quit. Have you got a match?"

The marshal struck a match. In the blue, sulphurous glow they gazed at the man lying sprawled on the floor. After a moment the marshal sighed, "Ain't nothin' some men wont' do to get theirselves killed, is there?"

Lamps were burning at the Empire station when Rian shambled into the yard. Justina heard him and came hurrying from the house, a lantern in her hand.

"Rian is that you?"

"Yes, ma'am. I think so," he said. He stood by the bench outside the station door; it looked so irresistible that he sank onto it with a sigh as Justina hurried up.

"I heard a story that there'd been a rockslide. I couldn't stand the suspense any longer, and I was just about to hitch—"

"Do me a favor," Rian murmured. "Don't ask me

anything for a while. Dan's all right. Everything's fine. If there's any whiskey around, I'd like some coffee with about two inches of spirits in it."

"Of course," she said. "I'm so glad you're all right. Nothing happened, then?"

"The whiskey," Rian murmured. "And then the coffee. *Then* the questions. In that order."

But when she returned with the whiskey, he was sound asleep in a sitting position, a weary smile on his face. She set the whiskey down, blew out the lantern, and, sitting on the bench beside him, took his hand and patiently waited for him to wake up.


The End